SOUL BURN

I. S. BELLE

Kindle eBook ASIN: B0DJHF4LVQ

KDP Paperback ISBN: 979-8-308349-52-5

IngramSpark Paperback ISBN: 978-1-067041-82-3

IngramSpark Hardcover ISBN: 9781-067041-83-0

CONTENT WARNINGS

Immolation, swearing, addiction, blood drinking, violence, murder, parental abuse, mentions of amputation, PG13 discussions of sex, implied off-page sex, animal death and injury (THE DOG LIVES, IT'S FINE).

Taking down the beasts will require every blade you have inside you.

Hone yourself well.

— Guide To Hunting The Accursed Vampyre, volume XXI

———

U STAY SOFT

— Kade Renfield's t-shirt

ONE WEEK before Kade Renfield died, he settled in for a quiet evening with his boyfriend.

Everything was set up: popcorn fresh from the microwave. A documentary paused on the TV. Theo on the couch, absentmindedly untangling a ball of yarn.

It was the kind of thing that drove Kade crazy, but Theo found it weirdly soothing. He'd been untangling a lot of yarn since he'd moved in. Cooking foraged mushrooms. Pruning the wisteria and rearranging old takeout containers under the sink. Not being able to sleep gave him a lot of time on his hands.

Theo spoke up from the couch. "Sure you don't have FOMO from missing out on the Founder's Day party last night?"

Kade snorted. "Would I rather crash a party no one wanted me at, or spend the evening watching *MASH* reruns with my boyfriend? Huh, let me think. *No.* You?"

"I don't really care about that stuff anymore," Theo said. He lowered his yarn. "God. Last year it was so important that everything was *perfect*."

He smiled bitterly. It was the anniversary, he'd reminded Kade last night. One year since Theo died. Which meant they had two weeks until the ritual night rolled around again.

Kade swallowed. They weren't talking about it. Not tonight, anyway. Tonight was a movie night. Kade would eat popcorn and knit, Theo would tell him fun facts about plants. Maybe later they'd both put gloves on so they could hold hands.

Kade's bare fingers flexed around the popcorn bowl. He never knew how much he'd want the simple luxury of holding his boyfriend's hand, no fabric in the way. Milly and Kade had been looking into a way to nullify the ritual: if Theo and Kade weren't the lock and key, then Victor couldn't get Cyth out of her burning prison. But it also meant that Kade could finally kiss his goddamn boyfriend without risking third-degree burns. He knew he should be more excited about Lock not getting destroyed.

But mostly he was excited about the kissing thing.

Kade still hadn't told Theo about his current plan. He was saving it for when Theo was in a good mood.

"Alright," Kade said, falling into the couch. "Let's learn about plants. Woo!"

Theo snorted, letting Kade sling his skinny legs over

his jean-clad knees. "You don't have to pretend to be so excited."

"What's not exciting about carnivorous plants?" Kade twisted to look down the hall. "Where's our favorite girl?"

"Don't tell Liss you said that."

"Liss understands." Kade whistled. "Sparky! Here, girl!"

Silence.

Theo looked up from his ball of yarn and frowned.

Kade's heart plummeted. "What?"

"One second." Theo closed his eyes.

Kade's heart sank even lower as he watched the line between Theo's blond brows deepen. They'd been working on the link between Theo and his hellhound ever since she obeyed Victor during that awful fight. If Theo focused, he could sense where his dog was. Judging by how long Theo was searching, Sparky wasn't anywhere close.

Kade sighed, lifting his legs off Theo's lap. "I'll go get the keys."

They left the plant documentary on pause. This evening was still for them, no matter what lay ahead.

Kade drove. He needed practice. He was going for his unrestricted license next year, and he was much less confident than Theo behind the wheel. It was one of the many things he had on this year's to-do list: get better at driving. Pass sophomore year with a B average. Save some money. Theo was trying to get him a job stocking shelves with him at the grocery store, but no one was eager to hire the teen who had been arrested several times and had a history of getting into fights, even if Theo vouched for him.

Kade was setting up for his future. He was *going* to have one, even if every part of him told him he was doomed. That he'd been doomed his whole life. It was *in* him, as deep and crucial as his bones.

Theo pointed. "That way."

Kade jerked the wheel. They both grimaced as Theo's Lexus veered around the corner.

Theo opened his mouth.

"Go slower on corners, I know," Kade said.

"That's not it," Theo replied. He peered out at the trees streaking past. "I just...assumed she was heading to my old house."

Kade grunted. He'd been as surprised as Theo when they'd turned that corner.

"Guess she's got somewhere else to be," he said quietly.

Kade brought the Lexus to a rumbling stop outside the Fletcher house.

Kade peered up at the big house, dread brewing in his chest. "They didn't dognap her, did they?"

"She doesn't feel stressed." Theo cocked his head, listening.

Kade whispered, "Are they home?"

"Don't know. I can't tune into them like I can to you." Theo climbed out of the driver's seat. "Come on. The plot thickens."

Kade huffed a laugh. A year ago, he would've been excited, another page turning in the story. But a year ago he thought this was a fun story they'd stumbled into, not a grim tragedy they were trapped in.

Theo cupped his hands around his mouth and whispered, "Sparky! Come here, girl!"

A happy woof echoed through the warm evening air.

Theo shushed her. Then he blurred into motion. Kade blinked twice and his boyfriend was standing in front of him, a dirt-smeared Sparky in his arms.

Kade scratched her muddy muzzle. "Naughty girl. We could be learning about venus flytraps right now and instead we're chasing you down. Are you happy with yourself?"

Sparky wagged her tail, bumping Theo's chin.

"Rotten little shit," Kade mumbled fondly.

Theo kissed Sparky's head. "Alright. Let's drag the runaway back home and—"

He stopped. He was staring at the house. No, scratch that—he was staring *past* the house, watching the greenhouse tucked into the mouth of the forest. The heavy padlock on the door was gone, the door half-open.

Aaron Fletcher ran into view, and even from this far away Kade could tell he was swearing. He caught sight of the boys and froze.

His remaining hand tightened around the trowel he was carrying. When he came back to school after the fight with Victor back in autumn, one hand was swathed in braces and bandages, and the other hand was gone. In its place was a stump, his sleeve buttoned over it.

Kade nudged Theo. "Come on. We have a hot date to get back to, remember?"

"What? Right." Theo spared one last look at the frozen shape of Aaron in front of the greenhouse. Then he turned back toward the car, Sparky wriggling in his arms.

Kade followed, his gaze stuck on Aaron's dirt-streaked trowel. Aaron didn't seem like the type to do his own gardening. Then again, maybe they'd fired all the help. The Fletchers had gotten increasingly insular since Mr. Fletcher died. Former social butterfly Mrs. Fletcher glared if fellow moms tried making small talk at the supermarket. Aaron quit the basketball team and even stopped wearing hair gel, hair flopping sadly as he slouched alone from class to class, his stump hand hidden in his sleeve.

Kade would feel sorry for them if they weren't such assholes.

. . .

The first thing Theo did once they got through the door was kneel and press his forehead to Sparky's.

"No running away," he told her. "You live here now, alright? *Home*."

Sparky barked. Then she licked Theo's face, smearing yet more dirt, and scampered down the hall toward Aunt Sundance's room.

Kade grimaced. His hand twitched toward Theo's face, wanting to wipe it clean. For a moment he let himself entertain the fantasy that they were normal boyfriends, and Kade was able to do something so simple as touch his cheek. Then he curled his fingers into a fist.

"The venus flytraps await," he said, gesturing toward the paused TV.

"Great," Theo said, with such a forced air of excitement that Kade could hardly believe this was the same guy who cried over venus flytraps during class in freshman year. He'd said it was allergies, and because he was Theo Fairgood—basketball star and all-around golden boy—everybody believed him. But now Kade knew the truth: under that asshole jock facade lay a soft heart that cared deeply when people tricked venus flytraps into closing for their own amusement, even though it used up precious energy and could eventually lead the plants to die.

Kade had fallen in love with him all over again when Theo admitted that. He'd had to excuse himself and hide in the bathroom, silent-screaming and punching the air until he calmed down.

Kade tugged on Theo's shirt. "New plan. Let's do something fun. Even *more* fun than watching an old man talk about carnivorous plants for one-point-five hours."

"Like what?" Theo said, pursing his lips in that specific bend that only happened when he thought Kade was about to make fun of him.

Kade was going to have to let him down.

"Remember when we watched Peter Pan?"

Theo blinked. Kade could almost see his mind work, trying to figure out what Kade was getting at. They both had crushes on Peter *and* Wendy as kids? Kade's long rant about color theory?

Then it clicked. Theo smiled, and there was nothing forced about it.

Kade stood at the end of his bed, grinning. "Ready?"

Theo nodded. He was hovering near the ceiling above Kade, arms outstretched. Waiting for Kade.

Kade sucked in a deep breath and closed his eyes. "To Neverland!"

Then he leapt. For a moment there was nothing, just gravity. He sailed toward the ground—

—then jerked, breath whooshing out of him as Theo grabbed the back of his shirt. He clenched his stomach muscles like Theo had told him. Then he held out his arms, wobbling. "Fly me around!"

"Bossy," Theo said. But he was smiling when he glided around the room, Kade dangling below him.

Kade giggled. If only everyone at school could see him now: Kade "Monster" Renfield, renowned for snarling at teachers and crashing house parties, reduced to a giddy mess by a fulfilled childhood dream.

Sparky whined, scratching at the door.

"Sundance is on a walk, she'll be back soon," Theo called. "And she'll be mad you ran away again!"

Sparky's whines grew even more pathetic.

"You're too hard on her," Kade scolded, unable to keep the laugh out of his voice.

"You're too soft," Theo replied. He pulled Kade higher, cautiously winding his arms around Kade's chest and embracing him from behind. They'd shoved gloves and scarves on before they started. Long sleeves, long pants, high socks: anything to protect Kade from Theo's burning touch.

Kade twisted to press his cheek into Theo's scarf, thinking about what Theo had said when Kade knotted it around his neck.

This will suck for you in the summer. As if he was sure they'd even be here for summer. If they didn't stop the ritual, Theo would be alive—well, he'd be *around*—and Kade would be a pile of ashes.

"Careful," Theo said as he pressed behind Kade, holding him afloat. "No more face burns."

Kade rolled his eyes. "That was *one* time, and I was

still half asleep. *Excuse* me for taking advantage of what I thought was a dream."

Theo snorted. He'd shoved Kade away as soon as he realized what was happening, but it still ended up with Kade getting a burn on his nose that stung so much he cried while Theo healed him.

"Sounds like a good dream," Theo said quietly.

"It was," Kade replied. It had melted into the visions he'd been having of their past selves—longing glances and meetings by the lake, knowing looks shared across the street. Kade preferred those dreams. Much better than the confusing flashes of blood and fear and horrible, horrible pain. Kade still hadn't seen how their story ended. But he could guess.

Kade twisted further in Theo's arms. "Do you—?"

He'd been about to ask whether Theo could dream, and whether he thought he'd get visions too. But then his forehead bumped into Theo's cheek, and he cut his words off with a sharp yelp as his face burned.

"Shit," Theo spat. He loosened his grip, almost dropping Kade before he let them both fall to the bed with a heavy thump.

Kade's eyes watered. He yanked his scarf off, trying to tamp down the raging embarrassment. Stupid, stupid, *stupid*. Theo *told* him to be careful. They were having a nice night, and Kade had to go and screw it up.

"I'm fine," he said, a traitorous tear slipping down his cheek. "It's okay."

"Shut up and let me heal you," Theo said, ripping one glove off.

Kade squeezed his eyes shut. Theo touched his forehead, and the pain flared before ebbing away to a sting, and then finally to nothing.

Kade opened his eyes. "What do you think, doc? Will I live?"

"You'll live," Theo replied, watching Kade with that reserved guilt he always got after he burned Kade by accident. But there was something beyond the guilt that made Kade suspicious.

He raised a hand toward the spot Theo had healed. "What? What is it?"

Theo gestured at Kade's forehead. "You, uh. You burned a streak into your eyebrow. Hair didn't grow back."

"What?" Kade launched off the bed and stumbled over to the full-length mirror he kept propped up next to the sewing machine. There was a jagged gap in his eyebrow, much like the scarred cartoon characters that Kade loved as a kid.

Kade whooped. "Holy shit! I should've thought of this ages ago. This is great, I look *awesome*. Am I scarier now?"

"You do look pretty badass," Theo agreed. "But no. You don't look scary. You look like Kade."

Kade welled up. He'd never heard anybody say his name like that before: soft affection, deep reverence, incredible hunger. Like Theo had tasted him down to his marrow and still wanted more. Like Theo had *seen* him, blood and flesh and sinew, and thought his jagged mess was beautiful.

"I love you," Kade said. His voice was high and squeaky and mortifying.

Theo blinked. "What?'"

"Shit," Kade said, heart racing so loud Theo could definitely hear it. "Never mind."

Theo shook his head, caught between disbelief and amusement and some third thing that was soft and tender and broke Kade's heart a bit.

"I love you too," Theo said. Rushed, easy. Like he'd been waiting for a while.

"Oh," Kade said, sagging. "That's...that's fine then."

Theo took a hesitant step closer. "Are you okay?"

"Yeah," Kade croaked. He scratched his healed forehead, stroking the new line in his eyebrow. "Just thinking."

Theo waited. Sometimes he pushed, but the longer he knew Kade the more he'd cottoned onto the fact that Kade was physically incapable of stopping some things from coming out of his mouth, and if you gave him long enough it would spill over.

Kade sighed. "You know how in a story there's, like, rising tension—"

"Please don't explain story structure to me again," Theo said, a wary smile tugging at his mouth. "I know you really liked that *Save The Cat* book."

"No, I mean...things get better before they get

worse. A rise before the fall." Kade tried to find a throughline to grab onto, something to form a straight line out of his whirling thoughts. He'd been mulling on this for months now. He needed to say it right.

"Theo, my life is pretty great right now. My grades are good, like *actually* good. I have friends. I've been drinking way less, I haven't gotten into a fight in months. I have an amazing boyfriend, even if we can't make out. This is the happiest I've ever been! And the happier I get, the more I—" He stopped. Tonight was supposed to be about them. Not about the dark fate dangling over their heads, waiting to come down and crush them. But maybe they couldn't avoid it.

"I'm just not looking forward to the part where everything goes to shit," he blurted. "And I should...I should really tell you..."

Theo was already shaking his head. "We're gonna be fine. This isn't a sad story."

Kade scoffed wetly. "It was last time!"

"They weren't us," Theo argued. It was a constant point of friction between them: Kade thought they were new versions of two boys who died centuries ago, and Theo insisted that he was the only Theo and Kade was the only Kade. They weren't *copies* of people who died generations ago. They were *people*, full stop.

"Everybody says I'm going to die," Kade blurted, unable to stop it. "Even if you make it, I die. Either you kill me to stop the ritual, or you get forced into doing the ritual and *that* kills me—"

"We're going to get out of this," Theo insisted. "Together. Okay?"

Kade didn't believe. But he hoped.

"Okay," he muttered.

Theo touched Kade's cheek with the hand still wearing the glove. It was the yellow one, bobbly and terrible from Kade's first attempt at knitting. Even after Kade knitted him new ones over the winter, those yellow monstrosities were still Theo's favorite.

"Good," Theo said quietly. "Now, what were you going to tell me?"

"What? Oh." Kade chewed his chapped lips. He would wait, he decided. At least until they saw Milly next.

"Nothing," he lied.

KADE SHOOK his head with a scoff as he sat down with Theo at their new cafeteria table.

"They just can't keep their eyes off us," he said flatly.

Theo looked up just in time to see several kids turn away hastily.

"New world order," Kade muttered in that faded British accent Theo had loved even before he knew him. "About time they got used to it."

Theo nodded. It was still an adjustment: Theo had spent his whole life getting friendly waves from teachers when he walked into class. Gleeful nods from his classmates and high fives from his teammates. People said hi to him in the street and held the door open for him.

Then his dad died. Theo quit basketball. His dad's grave got mysteriously robbed. His mom went on an 'extended holiday' and Theo moved in with *Kade Renfield,* of all people. He got a night shift stocking shelves at the local grocery store and some people swore they saw him running through the woods on the nights he wasn't working: barefoot, no moon to light his way. Not to mention the whole mess with Aaron.

Theo didn't get waves anymore. No nods or greetings or held doors. The sympathy about his dead dad and suspiciously absent mom had dried up pretty fast since he came to school wearing Kade's *U STAY SOFT / U GET EATEN* shirt.

But as long as he had a few people in his corner, he didn't mind that most people avoided his gaze in the hallways.

He *did* mind that most of the town thought that Kade had 'corrupted' Theo, and they wanted to make their dissatisfaction known. Theo stuck by Kade's side whenever he could, but sometimes people got sneaky. And *other* times people were just stupid. Like Finn Harley, Theo's old teammate who excelled at jump shots and absolutely nothing else in life, shoulder-checking Kade so hard that Kade went sprawling onto the cafeteria floor.

"Oooh," Finn sniggered. "Watch it, Monster. I think you caught me with your claws."

Kade bared his teeth at him and hissed. It was less fierce than usual. He'd admitted to Theo during a sleepless winter night that he was getting really, *really* tired of the whole 'Monster' thing. It started out as a way to spite people: *you think I'm a monster? I'll show you my goddamn teeth.* But that was getting old. Kade wanted to be something else now, and he hated that this town wouldn't let him.

Finn's smirk dropped off his face when Theo picked him up and slammed him into the wall.

The cafeteria fell silent. Everyone looked up to watch Lock's former golden boy stick up for the boy he'd once tripped in these very halls.

"He's *growling* at me," Finn protested, with the guilty squirm of someone who hadn't seen Theo when he shoved into Kade. "You're defending him, dude?"

Theo's hands creaked in Finn's letterman jacket. He thought about how easy it would be to lift Finn into the air. He could rip him apart without even trying. He wasn't *going* to. But he *could*.

Dad would be proud, he thought as he watched a drop of sweat slide down Finn's neck. Unfortunately for Victor, Theo had given up on making him proud when the requirements included hurting Kade.

"You want to know something about growling, Finn?" Theo asked. "Animals do it to warn you. When they want you to go away. When an animal *doesn't* growl —that's when you should be worried."

He leaned in. Finn flinched.

"Finn," Theo said softly. "Do you see me growling?"

Finn shook his head.

"If I let you go," Theo continued, "are you going to play nice?"

Finn nodded.

"Good," Theo said. He let go of Finn's jacket,

pretending to brush it off as he stepped back. "Don't come near him again. I'll know."

Finn swallowed. Theo listened to the spit drag down his throat, blood rushing through his veins. Listening in on people's insides usually meant he'd gone too long without feeding. When was the last time he ate?

He turned back to Kade, who was on his feet again. Theo had expected him to look triumphant. But he mostly looked uncomfortable: narrow jaw clenched, skinny shoulders high. Like he wanted this to be over with already.

"You don't look tired," Finn said.

Theo sighed. "What?"

Finn shrugged. He glanced over at his teammates, who were all over at Theo's old table pretending like they weren't watching. No one had come to Finn's aid when Theo slammed him into the wall.

"Just expected you to look tired," Finn said with the jeer of somebody who knew this was either going to be great or send him to the nurse's office.

"Working nights," Finn continued. "Going on all those runs through the woods. You didn't run into Skeeter that night, right? At the Founder's Day party?"

Theo frowned. The air in the cafeteria had gone even more still than before.

"I didn't go to the party," he said. "Why? What happened to Skeeter?"

Finn's bravado dimmed. Theo could smell the nervous sweat under his armpits. For a moment he thought Finn was going to continue, but then Finn looked around. Saw how many eyes were on them.

"Uhhh," Finn said. "Never mind."

Theo watched him stalk out the cafeteria doors, ignoring the twinge of dread in his stomach.

He headed over to Kade. "You okay?"

"I'm good," Kade said. But he still had that tightness about him, eyes tracking like he was waiting for the next attack.

Theo squeezed his hand. Kade wore gloves most of the time now: knitted gloves, sheer gloves, black leather gloves with red hearts on the back. Theo stared at them often, hoping Kade would touch his face, maybe push a hand through his hair. It happened sometimes, mostly when Kade was blissed out mid-bite.

Kade squeezed back, some of the tightness seeping out of his shoulders. "I'm fine. Quit looking at me like that."

"I'm not looking at you like anything," Theo insisted, keeping hold of Kade's hand as they sat down at their corner table. He'd made Kade hide in the back-seat and duck into bathrooms to talk to him in public—he had a lot of PDA to make up for.

Kade picked up his fork. "Can I have your brownie? They gave me the corner slice."

"I think I can spare it," Theo said dryly.

Kade stole the brownie off Theo's tray, eating it off his fork like a hunk of meat. "What were they saying about Skeeter?"

"I don't know." The back of Theo's neck prickled. The normal cafeteria chatter was back, but under it were whispers, numerous and hushed. Theo only caught snippets:

...can't believe...

...thought Theo was gonna tear into him...

...woods, right? I heard her parents said...

Before Theo could home into one conversation, Felicity slid noisily into the seat beside him, her scuffed sneakers knocking into his ankles. Last year she said she'd rather be caught dead than wear sneakers outside of the gym. Now she was wearing them four days out of seven. She still wore makeup, but it was less soft. No more glow. No pinks. Now she was all dark reds and steely silvers, painting her eyeliner into savage points and cutting holes in her tights.

"Sick eyebrow gap," she told Kade, digging into her meatloaf with a zeal Theo had missed during her model years. She took out a short vine of fire eye and started twisting it around her fingers, a habit she'd picked up since autumn.

Theo eyed it. "Can you not do that when I'm around?"

"What? It's not touching you." Felicity dangled the vampire-burning vine over Theo's hand, like she was going to scorch him with it. "Kade has some in his pocket right now!"

"For emergencies," Kade said. "And I don't get it out when Theo's right there."

"You're such a baby," Felicity said, tucking it away. The movement made her sleeve rode up to expose a bandage around her forearm.

Theo snagged her arm. "What's this?"

Felicity grinned. "Mom's teaching me how to dodge. I am *not* good at it."

"I can heal it later."

Felicity pulled her muscled arm out of his grip. "Cluck at someone else, mother hen. I told you, I like the scars."

She fluttered her scarred hand at him. She'd gotten cut during their fight with Victor. Not even while doing anything cool, she'd complained when Theo healed her broken arm. After all those months of what turned out to be hunting training with her mother, Felicity had been caught with a piece of glass while shoving herself up after getting thrown into the wall.

Kade grunted into Theo's brownie. "Does your agency like the scars?"

Felicity gave a long and musical hum. "Been thinking I might drop them. They don't know what hot actually looks like."

"What? But it was your thing."

"I can have other things," Felicity said with the same razor smile she'd given him before she tried to do a backflip of a banister during her last house party. Luckily Theo had been there to catch her.

"Ooooh," Felicity said. "Corner brownie. Can I have it?"

"You're an even bigger freak than me," Kade told her, nudging it over. "Hey. Did something happen to Skeeter Bass at the Founder's Day party?"

"Skeeter?" Felicity snorted. "Who knows? Nobody tells me anything anymore. Maybe she smacked someone after losing in debate again."

"It's probably nothing," Kade said, gray eyes focused on his meatloaf. "Just assholes saying shit."

But Theo could see the worry he was trying to cover up. He had that same creeping dread as Theo. Something was wrong. The cafeteria was tense and drawn, and it wasn't because Theo shoved his old teammate into a wall.

Theo ducked his head and tuned into the whispers. Waiting for the jumble to turn to something that made sense.

...said she ran away. As if Skeeter would ever do that. She had perfect attendance, she was going to win an award for it...

...cops aren't looking into it? What's it going to take before...

...this town's going to the dogs...

"Oh look," Felicity said. "My ex is coming over. Hi, ex."

Theo's head snapped up.

Aaron came to an abrupt halt in front of him, hair flopping weakly over his face. No eucalyptus hair gel to clue Theo into his approach anymore.

"Jesus," Aaron muttered. "Tone it down. Someone will notice."

Theo stared. It was the most Aaron had said to him since his first day back at school with his stump hand.

Theo had cornered him in the gym locker rooms and offered to heal the skin over the stump. Aaron had glared at him, eyes flat and blank. Then he'd eased his backpack on—slowly, carefully, hiding a wince the whole time—and stormed out without a word.

"Um," Kade said. "Sunshine? Kinda hurting my hand."

"What?" Theo looked. He was squeezing Kade's hand so hard the leather glove was creaking with pressure. "Shit. Sorry."

He let go, rubbing Kade's thumbs in apology. Then he looked up at Aaron. "Skeeter Bass is missing?"

"Wait," Felicity said. "*What's* happening?"

Aaron glanced at her with her red eyeliner and scuffed shoes, cut-off sleeves and unstyled hair. A fond look washed over his face, there and gone so fast that Theo almost thought he imagined it. When Aaron looked back at Theo, his face was all steel.

"Do you know anything about it?"

"No," Theo said. "Do you?"

"Oh wait," Felicity said. "He can't tell us. Because he's an idiot who voluntarily took some stupid family curse instead of eavesdropping at the door and letting his *best friend* fill him in after. Good job, babe!"

She flashed him a thumbs-up, and quickly turned it into a middle finger, her nail black and chipped. Kade had given her an inexperienced manicure at his house last week after she tried to teach him how to throw knives. Theo had done a lot of healing that day.

Aaron sighed. Another fond expression crossed his face: that specific fondness he got when she was shitting on him.

"Bye, Liss," he said quietly. He turned to leave.

"Wait!" Theo stood, stepping in front of Aaron so fast that Aaron gave him another warning look.

Theo lowered his voice. "We're running out of time. I *know* you don't want that. No matter what you feel about me, or about vampires, none of us want that ritual to happen. We could—"

"I'm not going anywhere *near* you." Aaron's face creased with such loathing that Theo stepped back. Then the moment passed, and Aaron lapsed back into his usual cool haughtiness. "You're poison. *My* family is going to fix this. Nobody else can."

He strode off, chin held high.

Felicity watched him go, chewing Kade's corner brownie. "What a poser. *My* mom gave up on that 'we're the only ones' shit right after I told her what Mr. Fletcher tried to do to Kade."

Kade grimaced at the memory. "Has she found a way to talk to you about any of it yet?"

"*I* want to try notes. But *she* insists her great-grandmother's sister died when she tried to do that with her fiancé. So." Felicity shrugged, wiping crumbs off her chin. "We know everything she does. Now we're just waiting on Milly to finish translating the rest of the prophecy."

Kade grunted and lifted a hand to scratch his head, where he was letting his hair grow out. Theo dragged his gaze from Kade's gloved fingers to the exposed skin of his wrist, blood pumping so loudly that it drowned everything else out.

"I think that's my cue," Kade said, voice breaking through the roar. "What do you say, blood boy? Time for a bathroom break?"

Theo blinked hard. The room was full of people, cramped and deafening.

"Unless you want Liss," Kade continued. "Less fuss. No healing after."

Felicity presented her thin wrist, like he was going to feed from her in front of the whole cafeteria. "Oooh, yes please."

Theo rubbed his forehead. Liss's blood was fine. Good. *Great*, even. But she wasn't Kade. Her blood didn't light him up inside. Didn't make him clutch her closer and breathe in her scent. When he fed from Felicity, it was just that: feeding. Fulfilling a biological need. When he fed from Kade, he wanted to climb inside his veins and stay there.

"No," he said, standing. "I want you."

For a moment Kade just sat there, staring up at him. He had this look on his face that Theo had seen more often in the past months: dazed, joyous, a little sad.

Like he was already missing the moment before it was over.

CHAPTER
THREE

KADE WOKE UP SCREAMING, head full of flames that had been smothered generations before he was born.

"Hey," said a voice that had been calling for him in the dream. "You're okay. I got you."

Kade cracked his streaming eyes open. Theo was leaning over him in his work uniform, his nametag wonky in that ugly two-ply shirt. Sparky sat next to him, panting worriedly.

Sundance's voice echoed in from the kitchen. "Are we getting attacked?"

"No," Theo and Kade called back. Sparky barked.

"Alright," Sundance called. "Well, better than an alarm clock."

Kade scrubbed his cheeks dry, trying to banish the last of the vision. "How was work?"

"Fine," Theo said. He paused, looking at Kade like

he wanted to sink down on top of him. Then he sat against the headboard and heaved Sparky into his arms. "Think I need to work less. Or act more tired. People get suspicious when I show up to school after too many night shifts looking this hot."

Kade laughed. "Sunshine. *Multiple* people saw you running barefoot in the woods at three a.m. They think I dragged you into a cult. Or we're werewolves. Or you killed your dad to absorb his life force and your mom found out about it so she fled town."

"*Please* don't update me on the town gossip," Theo said.

Kade tried to smile. The dream still had its claws in him, phantom sensations of flames crawling over his skin, Theo screaming his name.

Theo slid on his knitted yellow gloves and ran his hand through Kade's short hair. "They weren't having a good time, huh?"

Kade shivered, arching into Theo's touch. His mind ached with a memory that wasn't his own: two boys lying in a patch of pink flowers. Gloved hands drifting through hair, past and present bleeding into each other: they'd done this all before. Even when Kade was growing up thousands of miles away, Theo was here. *Lock* was here. Waiting.

Kade sighed. "Why don't you want to believe they were us?"

"Because they weren't," Theo said instantly. "*I'm* me. *You're* you."

"I *saw* them. I felt—" Kade paused to push Sparky away gently before she could lick his nose. "I felt their feelings, I heard their thoughts. It was *us*! What's wrong with that?"

Theo's fingers paused against his scalp. "I don't believe in fate. I don't believe anyone is destined, or—or doomed. I don't love you because of something that happened a hundred years ago. I love you because I love you. That's the end of it."

It was the most romantic thing anyone had ever said to Kade. He had to clench every muscle in his body so he wouldn't surge up and shove their mouths together.

It would be worth it, Kade thought as he stared at his gorgeous dead boy who had brought him knitting needles and dutifully helped with his homework and put himself in front of danger for Kade again and again. *I'd burn myself to the bone for one kiss.*

"Cool," Kade squeaked. "I mean. Thank you."

Theo's soft expression twisted with amusement. "You're welcome?"

Kade shoved himself up. "I'm...shower."

"You shower," Theo agreed, nodding sagely like Kade wasn't going caveman on him. "I'll make you guys breakfast in a second."

Kade stumbled into the hallway, reeling. He'd spent so long wanting Theo's full attention, wishing Theo would talk to him in the halls or let his guard down instead of leaning away. Now Theo was holding his hand where everyone could see it and saying *I love you* and bringing him breakfast in bed like something out of Kade's most pathetic dreams, and Kade had to run away so he could calm down.

He had his whole head in the fridge when Sundance came in carrying a collection of old mugs from her room.

"There you are. I wanted—" she stopped, staring. "Something interesting in the cheese?"

Kade shook his head, forehead still pressed against the cold plastic.

"Alright," Sundance said. She heaved her mugs onto the kitchen counter, sighing in satisfaction when none of them toppled into the sink. "Okay. I've been meaning to talk with you, and you're not allowed to run."

Kade was back on high alert. He yanked his head out of the fridge and whirled to face her. "But that's my number one survival tactic."

"You'll live," Sundance said dryly. She looked nervous, Kade realized with a sinking stomach. She was tapping her belt with an urgency that he hadn't seen since she gave him The Talk in middle school, which ended with him throwing himself out of a moving car. It was only going five miles in a parking lot, but still.

Sundance took a bracing breath. "You and Theo. You're being...*safe*, right?"

Kade stared at her, uncomprehending. She couldn't be talking about what he thought she was talking about.

"Like," Sundance continued. She pointed down the hall, toward his bedroom.

Kade let out a nervous laugh. "He can't touch my skin, so...yes? We can't...we're not..." He waved nonsensically, cheeks burning. "We *can't*."

"You can't touch skin, yeah. But there's still ways to..." Sundance grimaced, looking at the ceiling. "There are other ways."

"There are?" Kade said weakly. He felt like an idiot. In his defense, everything he'd done with Aaron had involved skin on skin. In his defense, whenever he thought about him and Theo together, he thought about third-degree burns. In his defense, he'd never considered doing anything further with Theo if he couldn't kiss him while it was happening.

Sundance opened her mouth.

"We can't NOT be safe," Kade blurted in a panic. "Literally! We can't! Dire, painful consequences!"

"I just don't want to take anyone to the emergency room," Sundance started.

"He'd heal me," Kade said desperately. "Not that... we aren't..."

His face burned. He reached for the fridge again. He was realizing several methods he'd overlooked, and he didn't want his aunt watching him while that happened.

Kade's bedroom door burst open. Theo blurred into the kitchen, Sparky galloping behind him.

"Milly texted," Theo said before Kade could shove his face into the cheese for a second time. "She wants us to come over after school. She finished the—" He stopped, some of the urgency leaving him as he noticed the strange looks on their faces. "Are you okay?"

"Yep," Kade said, strained. "We're great. Aunt Sundance, aren't we great?"

"So great," she said, examining the ceiling with an intensity he hadn't seen since she broke her favorite belt buckle and had to weld the whale back on.

Kade forced his mind back on track. Prophecy time. Today could be the day he told Theo what he'd been discussing with Milly. A failsafe. A way out, if they were right about this.

Theo wouldn't like it. But he'd see reason. At least, Kade hoped he would. They were running out of time to try anything else.

Milly's living room was the worst Kade had ever seen it. Coffee stains on the carpet, papers piled on every available surface. She'd taken all the photos off the furthest wall to construct a clue board. At the center were four ripped cards: DOG, RITUAL, REINCARNATION, CAROL. She had underlined RITUAL, while CAROL had a string of question marks after it and the least information. Overlapping red string connected the cards and a haphazard collection of notes. There was a new one Kade hadn't seen before: MISSING STUDENT, complete with a yearbook photo of Skeeter and a disturbing note that read: *(army? power source? food? sacrifice???)*

"How's Dungeons & Dragons?" Felicity asked as she settled on the couch beside Theo and Kade. She'd tried to get into it, but quickly gotten bored when Milly wasn't talking about her character: an orc bard with a lute that doubled as an ax.

"Hmm? Oh, it's on hiatus," Milly told them as she bustled around, putting water glasses on top of old dusty books full of languages Kade didn't understand. "Until the week after the ritual. Hopefully everything will have unfolded by then. Either we stop it and I can resume my campaign, or we don't stop it, and then we'll all have bigger problems."

She sat down heavily on the couch opposite them, heaving a notebook into her lap. She hadn't washed her hair in a few days, and Kade doubted it would get much cleaner in the next two weeks. When Milly got too deep into her latest translation, she forgot about boring stuff like hygiene. Her Dungeons & Dragons friends came over every few days to make sure she was eating.

"So," Milly said, taking a sip of water. Then she paused and took a larger gulp like her body had just reminded her that hydration was good, actually. She pulled the notebook open, leafing through the creased pages.

"The prophecy says what day it will happen," Milly read out. "It will take place after dark. And...well, you all know the ritual needs Kade to die."

She glanced pointedly at Kade, who quickly found himself the center of attention. Theo looked appalled; Felicity was smiling that sharp, sickly smile she got when something terrible was about to happen. Her broken-bone smile, Theo called it.

Kade said, "Before you get all weird about it, hear me out."

"Weird about it," Theo repeated, incredulous. "Kade. We're not *killing* you. I'd burn the town down myself before I let that happen."

"I know." Kade rested his gloved hand on Theo's leg. "Look, this is just...solidifying what we know. Right? Everyone's saying I have to die for the ritual to work. So me and Milly came up with a plan. A loophole, if you will!"

Kade had gone through a magician phase as a kid. He would've been happy without Theo ever knowing about it, but then Aunt Sundance had to bring out the photo album during a movie night. Kade had lost that plastic wand in his move to America and hadn't bought another one since. No top hats, no deck of cards. No rabbits. But as he bounded to his feet and threw out his arms, Theo and Felicity watching expectantly, he couldn't help but think: *abracadabra*.

"You," he told Theo, "turn me into a vampire."

Silence fell on the room. It was only broken by the soft glug of Milly downing the rest of her water and resurfacing with a satisfied sigh.

Felicity snickered. "You heard him. Get those fangs out, blood boy."

"Only he gets to call me that," Theo said distractedly, eyes still glued on Kade. "Kade, I'm not going to do that to you."

Kade groaned. "Come on! I'm *asking*. I'm *begging*, mate!"

Felicity's phone vibrated on the coffee table. She reached for it, keeping one eye on the boys like they were a reality TV show she had grown grudgingly invested in.

"It's the perfect loophole," Kade insisted. "I have to die for the ritual to work, but if I'm already—"

"Dead," said Felicity.

Kade wavered her away. "Okay, thank you Liss for that helpful addition."

"No," Felicity said, looking up from her phone. "It's Skeeter Bass. She's dead."

THEO KNEW he should be sad about Skeeter. And he was, sort of.

He'd be sadder, he told himself as they drove to the funeral home, after he finished reeling from Kade's proposition.

"I can *hear* your wheels turning up there," Kade said from the driver's seat. "It's not like you're killing me for *real*."

Theo took a deep, calming breath. Kade's soft metallic scent filled him all the way down to his bones. He'd gotten so used to it in the past year. Sometimes he wore Kade's shirts to work so he could breathe it in if his coworker asked when his mom was coming back or how he was doing after his dad passed. He'd duck his head into the neckline and inhale, sometimes for the first time all night. It usually set him at ease.

But not now. Not with Kade talking about his own

death, tapping anxiously at the peeling steering wheel of Sundance's secondhand car.

"Too wide," Theo said automatically as they swung clumsily around a corner.

"I know," Kade barked. He cleared his throat, thin fingers drumming up a storm. "I always thought I was doomed. Even before all this—it was like I knew. Like it had all happened before. It kind of *had*, with most of my family. Lead a piece of shit life. Die young. This doesn't feel like that."

A yellow glow from the streetlights drifted over his face. One good thing about being in the passenger seat: Theo could watch Kade all he wanted.

"If it works," Kade continued. "If it stops the ritual...you could touch me."

He swallowed. Theo watched his throat bob and thought about a phrase Kade had said about himself last year: *shaky guy. Loud heart.* Would he still shake after Theo turned him? It wasn't just a fear response. He did it when he was happy, too. Once, he started shaking when Theo was holding him at night—carefully, wrapped in a blanket so they wouldn't touch. Theo had asked what was wrong and Kade had shook his head, body wracked with trembling even as he grinned.

I just never thought I'd have this, he'd admitted.

Theo didn't want to lose that. Didn't want Kade to be still and cold in his arms. Then again—if it worked, then Theo could finally hold him properly. No blanket

in between them for safety, no evaluating every movement in case their skin accidentally brushed. No gloves.

Theo tore his gaze away. "Can we do it as a last
resort? Like, if it's the day before the ritual and we still
don't have a plan."

Kade drummed faster against the steering wheel.
Theo expected him to bring up how they were running
out of time, how the memories of those dead boys were
more vivid than ever, how much he wanted to escape
this sword of Damocles hanging over his head—a refer-
ence Theo only knew thanks to Kade's rambles as they
did English homework.

Kade sighed. "If it works, why wait?"

"If it *doesn't* work," Theo started.

Kade rolled his eyes. "Milly and I have been talking
about this for months. It's a classic loophole! Like in
Macbeth when the prophecy says no one can kill
Macbeth who was born from a woman, and the
cesarean guy does it because he wasn't technically
born!"

"I always thought that was a cop-out. How did you
almost fail English?"

"I have to die for the ritual to work. I have to burn
to death. But if I'm *already* dead, the ritual is screwed.
They can't finish that final step. Right?"

"I don't know!" Theo barked. He jolted as Kade
took a speed bump too fast. "I don't know how any of
this works. I just don't want to trap you with this."

Kade gripped the steering wheel, still recovering

from the speed bump. "That's our whole schtick! We're trapped together!"

"Not like this," Theo argued. "This is *permanent*. You can't take it back. Unless you kill me, which—"

"Isn't happening," Kade finished. His jaw flexed, his eyes fixed distractedly on the road ahead.

Theo cursed himself silently. Of course Kade would take that the wrong way. He was always waiting for people to run out on him.

"Not that *we* aren't permanent," he tried. Then he said the next obvious thing. "Like, I'd marry you."

Kade blinked. Blood rushed to his cheeks, delicious and distracting. His heart beat so fast Theo's mouth watered.

"Um," Kade said, strangled.

"Not *now*. When we're, like..." Theo's mind reeled, trying to think of a normal age to marry the love of your un-life. "...thirty. Oh hey, we're here!"

Kade stopped the Lexus with a screech outside of Hersay's funeral home. Theo got out and sped all the way across the road before he forced himself to acknowledge that Kade wasn't following.

He turned back to the car. Kade was still in the driver's seat, staring out at the road with dazed eyes.

"Kade," Theo called. "You coming?"

Kade looked at him. Cheeks still flushed, heart still going a mile a minute. Making Theo ache in a hundred ways that had nothing to do with the blood running through his veins.

"Yep," he squeaked, and stumbled out of the Lexus after him.

Hersay's had installed a security camera at the back door.

"About time," Kade said as they stood out of range, sounding almost normal after the fiasco in the car. "How many times have you been broken into, guys? Theo, are you going to fly up behind and smash it?"

He turned to Theo, who was crouching down to examine the flowerbed planted next to the parking lot.

"I thought you said their flowerbeds were boring and that you were going to seed bomb them," Kade said. "Are you seed bombing now? Is this really the time?"

"They're still boring," Theo replied. He straightened, flipping a rock in his hand. "Stand back."

Theo slung the rock into the security camera, which went crashing to the ground in a shower of metal and plastic.

"*I* would've flown up," Kade muttered. "But I guess that's cool too."

Theo broke the door handle with one sharp tug. They'd installed a new lock. It looked fancy. Theo felt a little guilty about their previous two break-ins as he kicked the broken metal out of the way. He ushered Kade inside and closed the wrecked door behind them.

"Ah," Kade said. "Memories. What do you think, will we be doing this again a year from now?"

"I hope not."

Kade went over to one of the storage fridge doors and plucked the CRACK A COLD ONE magnet off.

"Souvenir," he explained when Theo gave him an incredulous look. "In case it really is the last time."

Theo was filled with a strange melancholy. Then he remembered he was standing in a funeral home scoping out the dead body of his classmate, and he sobered.

He followed his nose to the nearest body fridge. "Ready?"

Kade made a face and nodded.

Theo pulled out the tray.

Skeeter Bass's eyes were closed. Her skin was pale above the white sheet and her lips were parted. She'd finally gotten her braces off. Theo hadn't noticed until now.

Her neck had been torn apart. The scars she'd gotten last year were barely visible, the flesh open and bare. Pink tendons lay exposed and a hint of her jawbone showed through the skin. There was another deep, brutal puncture wound in her scarred shoulder. *Animal attack,* Felicity had told them drolly before they left.

Kade squirmed. "Man. Your dad's messy. *You're* always so neat."

"Thanks," Theo said quietly. He could feel Kade's gaze on him, worried he'd said the wrong thing. They didn't talk about Victor much. Even when they went to Milly's to try and come up with a game plan, they referred to Victor as Him. *When He comes back. When He tries something.*

Kade frowned. "Hey. Did her neck just...move?"

"What?"

Kade pointed. "There. Her neck looks different. I thought I saw—"

He broke off with a yelp as Skeeter's neck shifted. The skin was pulling together, Theo realized with dull horror. Healing. The tendons knitted together, skin sealing over it with a sickly wet noise. Her scars melted like they'd never been there in the first place.

Theo stepped in front of Kade, mind whirring. He didn't remember anything after he'd woken up dead. Didn't remember walking away from Kade or going feral on a deer. When Skeeter woke up, would she be herself?

Skeeter's eyes flashed open. They were liquid black.

"Oh shit," Kade whispered.

Skeeter sat up with inhuman speed. Her head jerked toward Kade, black eyes locking on him with a hunger Theo knew intimately. Her mouth filled with fangs.

Kade gripped Theo's sleeve, pulling desperately. "Oh *shit!*"

"Shit," Theo agreed. He held up his hands placatingly. "Skeeter. Hi. We don't know each other that well, but—"

Skeeter yanked herself out of the body drawer and lunged at Kade.

"Nope," Theo blurted. He blurred forward and caught her in midair. She hissed and bucked, swiping toward Kade. The sheet twisted around her in a demented toga, covering some but not all the important bits as she scrabbled.

Theo grunted, pinning her arms to her sides. "We can't put her in the Lexus like this."

"Got it," Kade said. He rolled up his sleeve reluctantly, face creased as he crept up to her.

Theo yanked Skeeter away from him. "Whoa, hey! What are you doing?"

"Calming her down," Kade said. "You have her, right? Chill out."

"*You* chill out," Theo muttered. He watched anxiously as Kade came closer, his beautiful wrist held out toward Skeeter's snarling fangs.

"Careful," Theo warned.

"Yes, *mum*." Kade lifted his hand closer to Skeeter and grimaced. "I don't trust those teeth. Can you bite me? I'll drip-feed her."

Theo's mouth watered. He motioned for Kade to come behind him, twisting his head so Skeeter couldn't reach before he opened his jaw.

"Hole punch," Kade muttered nonsensically. He pressed his hand against Theo's teeth. Theo bit down, lips peeled back so he didn't burn him.

"Ow," Kade said. "Thanks."

It was perfunctory, the most no-nonsense bite they'd ever shared. Theo licked his fangs as they went blunt, longing for Kade's bare neck. He'd fed yesterday, but he was always hungry when it came to Kade.

Kade held his bleeding hand over Skeeter's snarling mouth. For a moment she got even louder. Then she quietened, her struggle dying down as she tipped her head up to be fed. For a minute the only sound was the dull drip of Kade's blood falling into her mouth.

Finally, Skeeter's eyelids fluttered. She went limp in Theo's arms. She strained to keep her mouth open, but eventually even that went slack as she passed out.

Kade cupped his injured hand. "No fun without the venom."

Theo heaved Skeeter into a carry hold. Her mousy brown hair was wild with struggle, the sheet a bedraggled mess around her body. Blood smudged her chin and cheeks, even her nose from Kade's drips going astray.

Theo wiped her face with the sheet and looked at Kade pointedly. "Still want to be a vampire?"

Kade rolled his eyes and held out his injured hand. "Are you going to heal me or not, blood boy?"

KADE SHIFTED UNEASILY on Felicity's kitchen floor.

"Quit it," Felicity told him, muffled by a mouthful of bread and the crispest cheddar Kade had ever eaten. Beverly Sloan had given them cheese sandwiches and orange juice after they'd both bled helpfully into a glass for Theo to bring to Skeeter.

He rolled his bony shoulders against the kitchen counters they were sitting up against.

"Your elbow is digging into me."

Felicity dug her elbow into him even harder. Then she relented, scooching further away from him across the kitchen floor. It was checkered and polished and deeply ugly, further deepening Kade's loathing of rich people having money and then not doing anything interesting with it. Even the glass they'd bled into had been boring. Where were all the chipped mugs? The horrible thrift shop finds brought on a dare? Where was the *life?*

Felicity examined the bandage on her inner elbow. "There's no point giving your blood to a vampire if you don't even get a high from it. I get why you put up with burns."

Kade nodded, feeling the bandage on his own elbow. Theo had promised to heal both of them once he was back. But he'd healed Kade earlier, and he needed all the strength he could get in case Skeeter woke up feral again.

Felicity popped the last of her sandwich in her mouth and chewed loudly. She was wearing a lacy negligee two sizes too small and a baggy pair of sweatpants. Both were stained with egg and mouthwash. She had a zit on her chin, covered in white cream that she ordered from out of state. She used to glare at him when he saw her at anything under Peak Hotness, daring him to say anything. But the glares had gradually stopped. According to Theo, this meant she trusted him. That she viewed him as a friend, not just as Theo's boyfriend who she tolerated on hangouts.

Kade downed the rest of his juice and braced himself. Friends asked each other for advice. Felicity seemed like she'd even appreciate what Kade was about to say. He just didn't want her to appreciate it *too* much.

"Hey," he said slowly. "I don't want you to get all... *you* about this, but you can have sex without going skin to skin, right?"

Felicity stared at him, her blue eyes so bright with mirth that he immediately wanted to take it all back.

"Never mind," he tried, but she had already latched on.

"Oh my god," she said. She burst out laughing. "Are you two *seriously* not doing it? I thought Theo was joking! Get creative, guys!"

"Never mind," Kade said, louder. "Turning me into a vampire will nix the burning shit, and we won't have to worry about it."

She grabbed him, rubbing her dyed hair against his shoulder like a cat. "Nooo, I love it! *God.* Have you dumbasses never heard of dry humping?"

"*Yeah*," Kade snapped. "I did it with your *boyfriend.*"

This was a lie. If he'd done it with Aaron, he would've remembered it existed when he was pining over his and Theo's nonexistent sex life.

"Ex," Felicity reminded him, amusement not dimmed in the slightest. Kade had thought she would be put out by the discovery that her first and only serious boyfriend had been cheating on her for the first few months of their relationship. She'd definitely been *hurt*—he'd caught it on her face before she yanked up a sharp smile and made a stupid joke about greedy bisexuals that she insisted wasn't offensive because she was one—but she never threw that hurt back at Kade. A surprisingly mature move for a girl who purposely left chocolate to melt in the pocket of Kade's best jacket to get back at him for stealing a bottle of vodka from her party.

She continued, "What about a gimp suit? You're a fashion designer, you could make one!"

"Shut *up*," Kade hissed. He shoved a hand over her mouth. She licked it, then when that didn't work she grabbed his arm and twisted it. He tried to resist, but her muscles had only gotten more toned since she'd spent the last year combat training for several hours a day.

The living room door swung open.

"Skeeter's awake," Theo announced, looking mercifully unmauled. "She wants—"

He stopped, blinking at the scene on the kitchen floor.

Felicity let go of Kade's arm, which she'd twisted behind his back. "More blood? Happy to help. If she coughs up the venom."

Kade winced, stretching his twinging arm toward the juice they'd nearly knocked over during their tussle. "I'll pass. I'm over my daily withdrawal limit."

Theo watched him drink. He had energy drinks hidden all over Sundance's house. There were oat bars in the glove box of both their cars, and trail mix in the trunk. Kade had once caught him sneaking a bag of chocolate-covered raisins into Kade's backpack. Theo despised them, but it was one of the only snacks Kade actively sought out.

"She doesn't want blood," Theo said once Kade

finished the glass. "She wants to tell us what happened at the Founder's Day party."

Beverley Sloan was kneeling next to Skeeter's chair, untying the ropes.

"Just a precaution," she assured Skeeter as she pulled the last rope from her leg and went to stand next to her daughter. "You understand."

Skeeter gave her the rapid nod of a teenager who agreed automatically with whatever an adult said, no matter her personal opinion on it.

"Hi," she said to Kade and Felicity. "Thanks for the. Um." She nodded at their bandaged elbows.

"It's on us," Felicity said. "Next drink will cost you."

"Oh. Um. Okay." Skeeter gave her a bewildered smile and fiddled with the hem of her borrowed flannel shirt. Beverly had dressed her in Felicity's lazing-around clothes after Theo dumped her sheet-clad body in the living room.

"Can I talk to my parents?" Skeeter asked Theo.

"Later," Theo said. He gave her a reassuring smile, only a little strained. Kade was glad it was him squatting down next to her and not Kade, who couldn't squat that low anyway and would be doing a much worse job at pretending everything was fine.

Skeeter nodded. This meek attitude was the reason Kade was surprised to learn she'd smacked her opponent in debate club. If Aunt Sundance thought *he* was dead, Kade would start picking pockets and gnawing on the walls. He'd send smoke signals. He'd start hollering and wouldn't shut up until someone got word to her that he was alive. He'd *promised* to outlive her. He meant to make good on it. Even if he had to technically die to make that happen. She wouldn't care if he didn't have a heartbeat as long as he was still around.

"You said someone was calling your name," Theo prompted.

Skeeter swallowed. "Yeah. So I...I followed it away from the party. We've walked through those woods all our lives, you know? I thought I was safe."

She reached up and touched her neck. At first Kade thought she was groping for her cross necklace, which was long gone. Then he noticed her stroking fingers and realized she was searching for the scars Hawthorn had given her last year.

"Was it the same one?" she asked. "The one who attacked me last year—was it him?"

"No," Theo said quietly. "This was a different guy."

He ran a hand through his blond curls. He did that lately when he thought about his dad. Kade's fingers twitched at his sides, thinking back to Theo sobbing and chopping at his hair, the hair he shared with his father, blond curls drifting off the cliff onto the lake where Victor had dropped him.

Felicity thumbed at her phone case, which she'd been peeling on and off since Skeeter started talking. "They said there was a blood trail. That you ran from something. Did you karate chop him so hard he let you go?"

Kade gave her a sideways look.

Felicity snapped her phone case back on. "We took a self-defense course together in grade school."

Skeeter scratched absentmindedly at her neck, as if confirming the skin was still intact.

"I ran," she said. "While they were fighting."

"Who?" Felicity and Theo said in unison.

"The man," Skeeter said. "I don't know who it was. I was running. It was...*feeding* on me. It cut its hand, dripped some black stuff in my mouth. Then it just... stopped. There was an ax in his shoulder. It dropped me, and I ran. I heard them fighting, but I just kept running. Until I couldn't. The blood..."

She stopped, looking up at everyone with huge, wet eyes, dark liquid pooling at the corners. "You can reach my house through those woods. I kept thinking if I just made it to my room...like when you're a kid. Right? Turn off the lights and run to bed. If you run fast enough the monsters won't get you."

Kade tugged at his earrings uncomfortably. She probably had nightmares about the thing that attacked her last year. Everybody told her it was her imagination, an animal, it couldn't hurt her now. He imagined her mom hugging her in her dark bedroom: *you're safe, I have you. Nothing's coming to get you.* And then this.

"It was a vampire," she whispered. "Right? The story they tell on Founder's Day. The vampire under the town who wants out. That's real?"

Theo nodded. "The guy we're up against, he wants to let her out. Two weeks from now, he's going to try."

Skeeter nodded, dazed. "My family had stories. My Grandma—"

Her lips thinned. She let out a shuddery breath. "He asked where her journal was. Before the ax."

"Journal?" Kade asked, in what Theo called his eager puppy voice. *I can practically see your ears prick up,* he'd said once.

Skeeter nodded. "Grandma had this...*spell book.* She never called it that, but that's what it was. She never said anything about it, except that we were protectors, once. Insisted she couldn't say anything else. She tried, near the end. She tried to tell me. She touched my scars..." Her fingers stroked up and down her neck, tracing the lines where scars used to live.

Theo gave Kade a significant look. Kade felt the smallest spark of excitement—*the plot thickens!*—before reality set in. Like he'd once told Theo: stories were only exciting when you arrived out the other side. When you were in them, they were a dark jagged mess you couldn't see a way out of.

"So he wants a spell book," Felicity said, grimacing. "*That* can't be good."

Theo asked, "The man who saved you with the ax. Do you know if he got away?"

Skeeter shook her head. "He was bleeding. He had his hands over his face."

"So we're either waiting on a body," Kade said, "or a guy covered in bandages."

"Or another vampire," Theo added quietly.

Felicity whistled. "Another one? You guys will have to do rock-paper-scissors to decide who gets to kill your dad and turn human again."

"Your *dad*?" Skeeter said, appalled. "Wait, I can be human again?"

"We won't have *time* to talk about it, we'll be too busy trying not to get killed." Theo turned back to Skeeter. "Skeeter, can you remember anything else about him? What he was wearing, maybe how tall he was? Did he smell like anything?"

Kade opened his mouth to snark at Theo about how humans didn't go around noticing how people *smelled* in moments of mortal peril. Then he noticed Skeeter's vacant gaze. She was staring at Kade's arm again, eyes flickering black as she gazed at the spot of red on the white bandage.

Then she blinked hard, and the darkness was gone. "Sorry. What did you say?"

Felicity made a delighted noise. "*No more blood*, huh Theo? Dibs."

She tossed a defiant look at Kade, like she expected him to argue for it. Kade's knee-jerk instinct was to do just that: he'd been getting regular venom highs for a year now. If he went longer than a few days without, he started getting withdrawal symptoms. He'd only had to suffer through it once, before he and Theo were even friends, but he was always eager for more. Even now, with everything going on, Kade's first thought was to get her to back off. To take the bite for himself. Never mind he'd already given her blood twice today and he was feeling woozy. There was still that spark of annihilation in him, constantly looking for a pool of gasoline to throw itself in.

"Go for it," Kade said, ignoring the surprise on Felicity's face and the relief on Theo's.

He averted his eyes as Skeeter bit into Felicity's outstretched wrist. Felicity's face creased up in pain before easing into indescribable bliss. He would miss Theo's bites when he made Kade a vampire. He'd miss chocolate raisins and temperatures. He'd miss the sick relief of binge drinking and throwing himself into a fight he knew he couldn't win. But stopping the ritual and being able to touch Theo would be worth it.

Two weeks, he told himself as Theo unhooked Skeeter's eager mouth from Felicity's bleeding wrist. Then his problems would be over—one way or another.

"For a second I thought it was Finn," Skeeter slurred as the black faded from her eyes.

Theo frowned, holding Felicity up as she sagged from the venom high. "Finn Harley? Why?"

Skeeter wiped her mouth absently, licking blood off her hand.

"Because," she explained, "that's who called me into the woods."

"OKAY," Felicity said, as Theo peeled an apple for her in the cafeteria. "So either your dad has some voice mimicking powers we don't know about, or your old basketball teammate is in on the plan to make a bunch of vampire thralls."

"She's not a thrall," Kade pointed out, a term Theo only knew because Kade made him sit down for a vampire movie marathon during winter break. "She won't do what he says."

"Maybe she's a power source for the ritual?" Felicity suggested.

"Milly didn't find anything about power sources," Kade pointed out. "It's just something she wrote up when she was throwing around ideas about..."

He sent Theo a sideways look. Theo kept his head down, peeling another strip off the apple. *Power source* was the second most popular theory on why Victor was keeping Carol around, since Milly couldn't find any evidence of her being Cyth's reincarnation.

Theo looked over at Finn Harley, who was sitting at his usual table with the basketball team. It was infinitely easier to wonder if Finn was secretly helping Victor than dwell on his mom's probable death.

"He's probably just lying to her so she'll stick around," Felicity said with the airy lightness of someone who didn't really believe what they were saying. "Maybe she's not involved in the ritual at all. You said he really loved her. Right?"

Theo shrugged, watching Finn pick a shred of meatloaf out from his canines. Everyone was always telling him how sweet his dad was, how he doted on Carol. Taking her out for elaborate dinners after crushing a court case together. Keeping candy in his pockets in case she felt faint. *A sweet for my sweet*, like he wasn't keeping her blood sugar up so he could feed on her later.

Self-loathing washed over Theo as he remembered the chocolate bar he had in his jeans. That was different. He wasn't *manipulating* Kade. He wasn't lying to him. He was making sure Kade was okay because he cared about him, not because he was a portable blood bag.

"Sure," Theo said. "But I also thought he loved me, so. Maybe I'm just an idiot."

"You're not," Felicity said sharply. She'd always disliked his dad, and Theo could tell part of her was thrilled that she finally got to double down on it. She'd printed a picture of Victor on a knife-throwing target before she realized Theo didn't find it funny.

Kade's boot nudged Theo's sneaker under the table. Theo pressed back, the guilt still churning inside of him. He peeled the last strip off the apple, sliding the red spiral over to Felicity.

"Freak," Kade said as Felicity munched happily on it.

"Takes one to know one," Felicity said. She bared her teeth, poking the apple peel between them like a snake's long tongue.

Theo handed the peeled apple to Kade, only allowing himself a moment to watch Kade's lips brace against the white flesh before he turned back to Felicity.

"How's our new friend?"

"She's fine. Still freaked out, but fine. Playing a lot of chopsticks and getting annoyed when I inevitably win. Also she's pissed off that the last meal she had was this gross broccoli casserole her dad made."

Theo tried to remember the last meal he ever had. It was while he was setting up for the last Founder's Day party, so it would've been rushed. Leftover rice and frozen chicken tossed in the air fryer and a handful of whatever fresh vegetables were in the fridge.

Kade grunted. "That sucks. My last meal's going to be *great*. Comfort food the whole way down. Shepherd's pie. Scotch eggs. Bangers and mash. Shut *up*," he added when they both looked at him with badly disguised glee. "American food is just as crappy, it's just a different brand of crap! Stop putting sugar in everything! Why is your *bread* sweet?"

Felicity leaned over to Theo. "What's bangers and mash?"

"I don't know," Theo lied. Kade had shown him during a PowerPoint presentation of traditional British foods that ended with Kade instructing Sundance to wrestle Theo so he'd stop teasing him.

A loud bark of laughter made Theo look over. Finn Harley was slapping a choking teammate on the back, looking less like he was helping and more like he was enjoying the opportunity to slap the shit out of his friend.

Theo sighed. "I'm going to go catch up with an old teammate."

Kade made an uncertain noise into the peeled apple.

"Remember the best way to take a guy off guard," Felicity told him. She reached over to Kade, miming twisting his nipples.

Theo stood and pushed his chair back. "I'm not going to fight him. He'll know we're onto him. I'm just going to talk."

Finn was still smacking his friend on the back when Theo arrived behind him. A shocked silence descended over the table. Theo hadn't approached any of them since he moved in with Kade.

"What?" Finn asked. He turned to Bradley, the guy who'd been choking. "Why's everyone staring at me?"

Bradley, a senior with a bad elbow and a dangerous love for pranks that had ended in more than one ER trip, pointed timidly at Theo.

Finn twisted in his chair, giving Theo a baffled grin. "Oh shit, hey man! Uh, sorry about yesterday. You know how it is."

"Sure," Theo said dryly.

Finn patted Theo on the arm. "Knew you were cool, deep down. You're coming to my party, right?"

"Party," Theo repeated. "What party?"

"Oh, right." Finn patted Theo harder and stood up. He climbed onto his seat, then the table, narrowly avoiding several lunch trays as he spread his arms wide.

"CITIZENS OF LOCK HIGH," he yelled. "You are hereby invited to my birthday party, the biggest event of the year! Our usual biggest event of the year was sadly sullied by the death of our beloved classmate, Scatter."

"Skeeter," Theo reminded him.

Finn snapped his fingers gratefully. "Always in our hearts! Anyway, this party will rectify that. A monster masquerade, a proud celebration of our Lockian roots! Don your fangs and your masks and come as your favorite spook, specter, ghost or ghoul! Vampires preferred, obviously."

He fell silent, arms still spread, waiting.

Theo stared up at him, almost pitying. There was

something *missing* from Finn's rallying cry. Aaron and Theo always had an assuredness, a particular smooth cadence or a cocky tilt to their heads which let everybody know who was in charge.

Finn wasn't letting them know. Finn was *asking*: shoulders hunched self-consciously, a desperate glint in his eyes as he looked over the masked crowd. His arms were still open, like he was trying to make himself bigger. Trying to *be* bigger. A second-rate basketball player in a tiny town, making a deal with the devil so he could convince the world he was someone.

Nobody spoke. Finn glanced down at his teammates, panicked.

"Woo," Bradley said uncertainly.

Finn stabbed a finger at him. "Yeah, woo! Woo-*hoo*! Who's excited?"

A halfhearted chorus of whoops echoed around the cafeteria.

"Yeah," Finn said, climbing down to give Theo an anxious grin. He wasn't good at faking it. He never was, even back when he first joined the team. His nerves always shone through, no matter how much cockiness he tried to broadcast.

"So," Finn said, "you coming?"

"Sure," Theo said suspiciously. "Monster masquerade. Sounds great."

"I know, right?" Finn knocked his arm a third time. "You can bring Renfield along, just make sure he behaves himself. At least he'll have a good costume. Little freak looks like a vampire already."

Theo took a deep breath, reminding himself why he came over here. For information, not a fight. No matter how badly he wanted to shove Finn against another wall and tell him that whoever had a problem with his boyfriend had a problem with him—he had to hold it in.

A flicker of movement caught his eye.

Theo looked up. Aaron was slinking over to Theo's corner table, where Felicity and Kade were breaking the remains of the apple peel like a wishbone.

Theo walked off without thinking.

"I'll see you there," Finn called behind him. "Wear something cool, okay? I want it to be a photo op!"

Theo ignored him. He'd get back to Finn and his monster masquerade crap later.

Aaron was already at the table when Theo returned. Felicity aimed a razor-sharp smile sat him.

"Oh hey," she said to Theo. She pointed at Aaron. "Look, it's our ex again. Say hello, ex."

She motioned for Kade to say it. Kade stared determinedly down at his half-eaten apple, averting his eyes. None of them liked it when Felicity implied that Aaron and Kade were exes with a capital *E*, except Felicity, who liked it in the same way she liked pressing a bruise after a brutal training session.

Aaron had his hands in his pockets. Well, *hand*. He had his stump in his other pocket. Theo had rarely seen him do anything else with his hands since he showed up at school with one hand amputated at the wrist. His veins were still dark above the stump, faded black lines winding up to his elbow. Theo had gotten a glimpse during the one gym class Aaron attended with short sleeves. The next gym class, Aaron showed up in long sleeves and a glare daring the teacher to confront him about it. Nobody ever did. Aaron might not be popular anymore, but he was still intimidating. Just like Theo.

"Great to see you," Felicity continued, dripping acid. "Have you come to ask us to the monster masquerade? Apparently it's going to be a total photo op."

"No," Aaron said. Then he just stood there, jaw working. Figuring out a way to say it that wouldn't get him killed, Theo assumed.

"Heard Skeeter's funeral got delayed," he said finally.

Felicity sighed, biting another strip off the apple peel. "And you put the pieces together and want to know if you and your mommy need to put her down?"

Aaron's shoulders stiffened even further. "I—"

"Relax," Felicity said through a mouthful of apple peel. "She's safe."

"Safe," Aaron repeated flatly. He took a deep breath, like he was going to say something. Then he stopped. The barest smile strained over his mouth.

"Have a good lunch, Liss." He started to turn. Then he paused, eyeing Theo's tray, full of things he was going to throw out at the end of the period. "There are people starving, you know."

Theo wished he had a good comeback for that. He looked over at Kade hopefully, but Kade was aiming all his focus at the apple core he was gnawing. He'd been getting like that a lot in the past few months: less eager to snarl at people who messed with him. Less likely to throw himself into a fight. Theo was glad about the fighting thing, but part of him missed Kade throwing scathing comments at their classmates.

He waited until Aaron was out of earshot. Then he leaned in.

"We're still on for tonight," he said. "Right?"

Felicity flicked him a salute. "Operation Condolences is a go."

THEO WAITED on Skeeter's front porch.

Felicity and Kade looked at him expectantly. It had been a full thirty seconds and the doorbell remained unrung.

"I'm holding food," Theo pointed out. "You guys aren't holding anything."

"I still think we should break in," Kade grumbled. He held out a fist to Felicity. "Rock, paper, scissors? Friendly game of chopsticks? Unless you cheat, like Skeeter says."

"Ughhh." Felicity stabbed the doorbell.

Theo readjusted his grip on the lasagna, which was pleasantly warm in his hands. Sundance had helped him make it. And by 'helped,' he meant he let her grate the cheese. Sundance was a lovely person, but not a great cook. Theo needed the lasagna to be perfect for Skeeter's parents. It was the least he could do, after stealing their daughter's body and convincing her not to tell them she was still around. Only for another week and a half. But still—a week and a half was a long time to believe someone you love was gone.

The door stayed closed.

"Maybe they're not home," Kade suggested.

Theo concentrated. He could hear the muted tones of conversation from inside the house. A faint shuffling coming closer.

Kade asked Felicity, "How *do* you keep winning your chopsticks games with Skeeter?"

"I don't," Felicity said. "Whenever she wins, she insists I let her. I just nod."

Theo shushed them. The shuffling was getting closer.

The door opened. Mr. Bass blinked owlishly at them. He looked like the kind of guy Theo would've made fun of last year: polyester shirt, pocket protector, glasses magnifying his watery little eyes.

"I'm Theo," Theo said. "This is Felicity and Kade. We played chess with your daughter."

"Big chess fiends, us," Felicity agreed. "And chopsticks!"

Theo fought the urge to step on her foot. Her smile was *far* too wide.

"We wanted to drop by and offer our condolences," Theo continued.

Kade nodded silently. He'd mentioned in the car that it was better if he didn't say anything. He tended to offend townsfolk just by existing, and was convinced that talking would make it worse.

Theo held out the lasagna.

Mr. Bass stared at it like he'd temporarily forgotten what a lasagna was. Theo shifted uncomfortably, remembering the grief haze he'd plummeted into when he thought Victor had been murdered. Everything took a second too long to process. The world had dropped into another language and he had to stop to translate it before responding.

"Right," Mr. Bass said finally. "Come in."

He led them into the tiny kitchen. The peeling countertops were piled high with potato salads, deli meat, casseroles. Mr. Bass placed their lasagna on a tray of sandwiches. The sandwich filling oozed out, coating the bottom of Theo's lasagna dish in mayonnaise and cucumber.

"Right," Mr. Bass repeated. "Well. Thank you for coming over. Um. We appreciate—"

A voice rang out from the living room. "Who is it this time?"

"Chess fiends," Mr. Bass called back. "I mean, friends. Chess friends."

There was a pause. "Bring them in, then."

Mr. Bass walked wordlessly past them. He didn't look at them, and for a second Theo wasn't sure if Mr. Bass wanted them to follow. But it was that or stand here in a kitchen full of room-temperature food that was slowly but surely expiring, so Theo headed awkwardly down the hall after him.

"This was a bad idea," Kade whispered as he followed Theo. "They're going to throw us out. They're going to call the cops. We should've snuck in a window!"

"Which is *way* less likely to get the cops called on us," Theo whispered back.

Felicity shushed them. Less for silence, Theo was certain—since both Mr. and Mrs. Bass definitely heard it as they came into the living room—and more out of panic. Her smile was way too big yet again as she folded onto the couch opposite the grieving parents.

"I love your kitchen," she said. "Very sixties chic."

Theo nudged her, disguising it as an accidental bump as he sat down next to Kade.

"And we're so sorry for your loss," Felicity continued. "*God.* We're going to miss Skeeter so much. Playing chess with her was the highlight of our week. Right, guys?"

Theo and Kade nodded obediently. Theo could smell Kade sweating, but his worry at getting caught out was fading by the second. Mr. Bass was staring vacantly at Felicity, and Mrs. Bass wasn't even looking at them. She gazed into the middle distance, twisting her cross necklace absently. She had the same mousy brown hair as Skeeter, styled into a sleek hairstyle that hung down around her neck.

"Sucks that the funeral got delayed," Felicity said brightly. "Whenever it gets changed to, we're *there*."

Mr. Bass's knobby fingers tightened on his knees. "The cops aren't doing anything. The security cameras are gone, they said the thieves wore gloves, but there has to be *something*. I just don't know why someone would do this."

"Lock is a strange town," Mrs. Bass said. "These things happen."

Mr. Bass pulled himself out of his grief haze long enough to give his wife a baffled look. She didn't acknowledge him. She was staring at Theo with a strange, distant curiosity. Theo wondered how many rumors she'd heard about him.

"And how are you doing?" she asked. "Since your dad passed."

"Fine," Theo said, automatic.

Mrs. Bass nodded. "I thought it was very strange your mom didn't take you on vacation with her. You were always such a loving family."

Theo's throat tightened. If he got a C on a test, they made him stay up overnight and lift weights until he cried. If he lost a basketball game, they made him practice until he could barely move the next day. When he was six, he broke Carol's favorite glass and they made him pick up every tiny shard without gloves. There was still a dent in the living room ceiling where Victor had pressed him into the plaster.

Even with all that, the terrible truth was this: he

missed them. He missed coming home to his parents celebrating another case won. Dad ruffling his hair, no painful grip, just joy. His mom buying unripened bananas for Theo because she knew they were his favorite. Hikes on the weekends. Driving him to games, helping with his homework before they decided he was too old for it. Walking into the kitchen and seeing his parents waltzing to no music, so lost in their own little world they didn't notice him at all.

Kade touched his leg. Theo blinked hard. He couldn't tear up here.

Mrs. Bass was still watching him with that same detached curiosity. Like she couldn't decide which rumors she believed about him, but she had bigger priorities.

Theo cleared his throat. "Could I use your bathroom?"

He fled into the hallway, hand pressed to his cold chest.

Kade followed.

"Told them I needed your help taking my contacts out," he said with a wince. "What do you think? Are we screwed?"

"What, do you mean do they suspect we have their undead daughter hiding out in Felicity's living room?" Theo shook his head. "I think you could've danced naked in front of him and he wouldn't have noticed anything. The mom—I don't know what's up with her. Liss can take care of it. We have a spell book to find."

Kade's contact-less eyes lit up. Sometimes all you had to do was say a word that belonged in a fantasy video game and Kade would get as giddy as a middle schooler. It would've been cute, if Theo wasn't still rubbing away the horrible weight in his chest. He didn't want to think about his parents. Didn't want to think about Kade admitting that sometimes he wished he didn't have any good times with his dad, so it would be easier to hate them. Theo had so many goddamn good moments with his parents. Until Victor faked his death, they outweighed the bad so much that Theo could pretend the bad stuff didn't exist.

They headed down the hall, Theo mentally picturing the map Skeeter had drawn for them. *Grandma's room is the third door on the left.* Theo turned the doorknob. It stuck, like Skeeter had warned him it would. Nobody had been inside in years.

The door creaked open to reveal a bare white room. A single bed and a desk drawer and an empty bookcase tucked in the corner, bolted to the wall.

"There goes my first plan," Kade said, pointing at the empty bookcase. "What else is there to search?"

"You take the closet," Theo said, getting on his hands and knees. "I'll check under the bed."

He poked around the slats hopefully. Nothing popped out to reveal a secret drawer.

"I really should be under there," Kade said. "You have shoulders."

"*You* have shoulders," Theo replied. He liked Kade's thin, bony shoulders. He stared at them often, watching them strain through his shirts.

"You're *broad*," Kade argued. "Probably gonna get stuck down there and we'll have to break the frame to get you out." He squatted, meeting Theo's eyes under the bed. "Hello there. Stuck?"

The weight in Theo's chest didn't vanish, but it stopped feeling like Victor had him shoved into the ceiling, plaster cracking around his head.

"Not yet," Theo replied softly. He squeezed out from under the bed, scraping his shoulders against the bedframe. "Okay. I'm going to check the..."

He trailed off. There was an embroidery hoop hanging above the door. Plain white with simple black stitch in the center: WHEN THEY BITE US LET THEM CHIP THEIR DAMN TEETH.

"Oh *hell* yeah," Kade said, tracking Theo's gaze. He stretched up to reach it. His fingertips barely skimmed the bottom of the embroidery hoop. He turned to Theo with a comical pout. "Sunshine?"

"On it," Theo said. He drifted into the air and tugged on the hoop. It was bolted into the wall. Theo tugged harder. The embroidery hoop snapped off, the wood cracking around the nails.

Kade let out the world's quietest whoop. Tied to the back of the hoop was a thin, worn notebook. It had no title, but Theo knew what it was even before he landed on the floor and flipped it open: faded pages filled with sketches and writing so heavily cursive that Theo couldn't even begin to read it.

"They really should start teaching us to read this shit again," Kade said, swiping it out of Theo's hands. "I wasn't even sure that was *English* for a second."

He flipped through the pages. More spidery writing, more sketches. A familiar woman with sharp cheekbones and even sharper teeth, her red hair twisted in a plait around her head. A sketch of a dress—

Theo paused. There was something else tied to the back of the embroidery hoop. A small, dusty leather pouch, the drawstring pulled tight.

"Huh," he said.

Kade hummed, still examining the sketches. "What?"

"Found a pouch."

Kade gasped, snapping the spell book shut. "A *magic* pouch?"

"It looks magic-adjacent." Theo tugged the drawstring open. Dark dirt, something that looked depressingly like bones. And flower petals, which the dirt didn't stick to.

Theo took a petal out of the pouch, examining it in the dim light. They were so pink and plush they could've been plucked that morning.

"They should've rotted. This thing's covered in

dust." He examined the petal's diamond shape, going through varieties of pink flowers in his head and crossing out each one. "I don't think it grows in Lock. I don't recognize it."

"I do," Kade said quietly. He had that faraway look on his face that he often had after waking up from a dream: like time was unfolding on itself.

Finally, Theo realized: "The pink flowers you've been dreaming about!"

Kade nodded, dazed. "Should've rotted," he echoed quietly. "Long time ago. But they're still here. Still right...*right* here."

Theo swallowed. He hated it when Kade got like this, so far away Theo couldn't help him. Could only wait until he came back out.

"Kade?"

Kade blinked hard, and the unfolding expression was replaced by a shaky smile. "Are those bones? What kind of bones, do you think?"

He leaned in.

Something flickered past the window.

Theo grabbed Kade's sleeve.

"What?" Kade's fingers twitched, half an inch away from the bone lying at the top of the pouch.

Theo shushed him.

Kade sighed. "Everybody's shushing me today."

Theo shushed him again, urgent this time. "Something's out there."

Kade's uncertain smile dropped. He stepped closer as Theo swayed unconsciously in front of him, gaze trained on the window. There was no movement, just distant trees. But he'd been so *sure*. It was the flash of a wing, the hint of a claw. It had been paler than the moon, which was hanging almost full in the sky.

Kade whispered, "Is it—?"

"I don't know," Theo admitted. But there was this horrific bone-deep knowledge he hadn't felt in months. *I am his.* Victor was nearby. He could feel it.

But seconds kept ticking away, and nothing happened. The bone-deep knowledge started to recede. Did he imagine it? Sometimes he felt it when he was out in the woods. He'd be so *sure* he was being watched, but he'd never be able to hear anything. Never spot a sliver of white through the trees, never those terrible eyes melting into the same color Theo saw in the mirror—

"Theo," Kade said, voice soft with horrible understanding. "I think we're okay."

Theo shushed him again. There was a new sound coming toward them: footsteps in the hall. Felicity's light, athletic step trailing behind someone fast and determined.

"Shit." Theo whirled. The bedroom window was too small to get out. There was no way to pass off being in the dead grandmother's room as anything but suspicious or weird. They would have to lean into weird.

Theo messed up his hair. Then he shoved the book and the pouch down the back of Kade's jeans.

Kade squeaked. "What's happening?"

"Just go with it," Theo said. He wrapped his arms around Kade and dropped his chin on his shoulder, tilting his head so it looked like he was kissing Kade's neck.

Kade's pulse fluttered deliciously. He swallowed, that bullseye mole rippling with the motion, and Theo had to fight back his fangs. He'd never been this close to Kade's neck without sinking his teeth in.

He squeezed Kade's waist. Kade made a noise like he'd been punched in the gut.

The door opened.

"Oh," Kade said, high-pitched. "Shit."

Theo turned, trying to look guilty for the right reasons.

Mrs. Bass was standing in the doorway, her expression unreadable. Felicity arrived behind her, a terror-smile plastered on her face.

"Wow," Felicity said with a giggle. "Grief does such weird things, huh? You should've seen him after his dad died, he was dragging Kade into closets every five minutes. Let's go, you messed up lovebirds!"

"Mrs. Bass," Theo said, straightening his hair. "I'm so sorry."

Mrs. Bass watched Theo as they headed down the hall. He still couldn't tell if she was suspicious. If she was, it was buried under so many tangled layers of grief that it would take a long time to struggle to the surface.

Theo's dead heart twisted in his chest. Skeeter's parents wouldn't have to mourn for long. They'd get her back to them soon.

CHAPTER
EIGHT

"ARE you allowed to smoke in here, Felicity?"

Kade looked over at Skeeter, annoyed. Skeeter was interrupting one of his favorite boyfriend rituals. Smoking was one of the most intimate things he got to do with his boyfriend, full of indirect closeness and prolonged eye contact that made Kade's stomach swoop in shivery delight every single time. And here was Skeeter, ruining it with her questions.

"Officially? No," Felicity said from her seat next to Skeeter on the couch. "Unofficially? Mom doesn't care. Smoke away, boys."

Kade nodded in silent agreement. Theo was still breathing in, the tip of his cigarette flaring against his own. Kade couldn't stop thinking about Theo's arms around him at Skeeter's house, those big hands on his waist. Just like how Theo held him at night—with a sheet between them, of course.

Theo leaned back, his cigarette already half gone. He could breathe in for a long, *long* time. "How's the translation coming, Skeeter?"

Felicity snorted. It was *technically* a translation, but only because none of them could read cursive except for Skeeter, who was still having trouble deciphering the handwriting that was not, as they had assumed, her grandmother's. It was probably her great-great-grand-mother's, she had said when they handed it over. Maybe add another great on there.

"Um," Skeeter said, squinting at the faded pages. "There's a lot of stuff in here about Cyth. About getting her out of the coffin. It needs certain ingredients. A dress, a spear, and a flower that only blooms one week a year."

Kade made an urgent noise and turned to Theo. Theo already had the pouch in his hand, yanking it open to show Skeeter the impossibly plush petals.

"Oh," Skeeter said. She held up the spell book to compare the sketch: same diamond-shaped petal, same soft veins running through the middle of it. "That looks like it."

"So we need to find where they grow," Kade said. "Lucky we have a plant expert on our hands."

"I don't know," Theo said. "I really don't recognize it. What dress? What spear?"

Skeeter flipped the pages. There was the dress Kade had seen when he was examining it earlier: white and flowy with a fanged belt. Not the one he'd seen her wear in visions, but close to it. The spear was on the next page, short and barbed. The kind that hurt you more when you pulled it out.

"Does it mention anything about needing newborns?" Kade asked. "He turned you. He had to have a reason. Or anything about the pouch?"

"Um." Skeeter turned the book back so she could look at it. "This handwriting is really hard going. So maybe that's in here later."

Felicity tutted. "What's all this new shit? I thought he just needed you guys."

"This is good," Kade pointed out. "If we break the spear or burn the flowers, he's screwed. Until next spring, anyway. Right?"

"Sure," Skeeter said, sounding unsure. She dropped the book into her lap, twisting the pages anxiously. "Hey, when you said my parents were 'as good as can be expected,' what did that mean?"

Kade, Theo, and Felicity traded a look.

"They'll be really happy to see you're back," Felicity said.

Skeeter gnawed on her lip. "I just don't see why I can't visit. They can keep a secret. I feel really bad, letting them think I'm dead."

Kade tucked the snake-flower lighter Theo had gotten him back into his pocket. Smoke drifted up toward the Sloans' living room ceiling, and Kade watched it warily. Beverly Sloan didn't hate him, he was pretty sure. But she didn't like him either, and he wouldn't win any favors if she found out he was smoking in her house. It was the kind of thing he'd have done eagerly a year ago. But he was getting tired of daring people not to like him.

Theo was pacing now, tight circles in between the two couches. "This is useless. Even if we destroy all that stuff, we still have to fight him. I should be learning how to grow wings, get bigger, get *stronger*. Does it say how to do that?"

"I don't see why it would?" Skeeter said. "This isn't, um...a vampire how-to book? It's a spell book?"

"Right," Theo said. "Yeah. Right. Okay. That's... fine."

The cigarette burned down in his fingers. He often forgot about it. Like he was only smoking for the first part, where he got to lean in so close to Kade and breathe in, watching him with those big dark eyes.

"Not a problem," Theo continued, pacing faster. "We have one and a half weeks until the ritual and now we have some...some highest stakes *scavenger hunt,* like we don't have enough to deal with—"

"Theo," Kade tried. Theo was starting to blur.

"*What?*" Theo turned, superspeed elbow catching on a vase and sending it smashing into the wall. Ceramic went flying, embedding in the curtains and skidding under couches.

Skeeter yelped. Felicity let out a nervous snicker.

"Nice," she said. "I hated that one."

Theo gave her a tired glare and stubbed his cigarette out on his own hand.

Kade started toward a shard of ceramic. "It's fine. We can—"

"*Don't*," Theo snapped. "I can fix it. I broke it, I can fix it."

Something dark and defensive curled inside Kade, all fangs and snarling. If he got barked at, he barked back. That was how he'd lived his whole life. He reared up, ready to bare his teeth. Then he looked at Theo's wide, angry eyes and remembered that time Kade had tried to help Theo clean up a mug he'd broken in the sink. Theo had yelled at him, and Kade had yelled back, and Kade had retreated into the woods for a long walk with music blaring from his headphones. Theo had caught up to him five minutes later, fists clenched at his sides.

When someone tries to help after something like that, Theo had admitted, *it just feels like they're rubbing my nose in it. Like they're saying I broke something and I can't even fix it on my own.*

Kade stubbed out his cigarette on a glass coaster. "I'm going to get the vacuum."

He headed down the hall toward Felicity's laundry room, trying to smooth down the jagged edges that appeared whenever someone snapped at him. *You don't have to blow yourself up every time someone hands you a match,* his mum had said to him once while she scrubbed blood off his face. Ironically, she was quoting her own mother. The Renfields were a family of wildfires, handing down the blaze to the next generation.

Kade had barely stepped into the laundry room when Theo appeared in the hallway behind him, his hands full of vase shards, the spell book poking out of his jeans pocket. He looked like he wanted to have a serious conversation, so Kade cut him off before he could start.

"We're taking the spell book to Milly after all?" he asked, gesturing at the book peeking out of Theo's pocket. "Told you we should give it to her. She translates dead languages on pages that have been rotting for centuries, she can deal with Skeeter's great-grandma's handwriting."

"What? Sure." Theo caught a vase shard that was trying to escape his grip. "Look, I'm sorry."

Kade stooped to pick up the vacuum cleaner. "It's fine."

"No," Theo said. "I'm sorry I said I'd marry you. I freaked you out."

Kade winced, tightening his hands around the vacuum handle. He had hoped they would stumble past that and forget to mention it until they knew if they would survive until summer.

"You didn't—"

"I *did*," Theo said. "I saw your face."

Kade turned to face Theo, vacuum cleaner banging

against his knee. "You didn't freak me out. I want...I'd *like* to marry you one day. I just can't see it happening."

"Oh." Theo's jaw tensed. Kade could see him doing the same thing Kade had done after Theo snapped at him: trying to read between the lines. Trying to glimpse something that didn't hurt.

Kade squirmed. He wanted to explain it: he had thought about them dying tragically in each other's arms a hundred times. He hadn't thought about *marriage*. The idea made his stomach twist with delighted horror. They'd only started saying *I love you* this week. The idea of marriage freaked Kade out even more than dying tragically. He'd never envisioned life after high school. Not seriously. He'd had pipe dreams of fashion school, bright cities, likeminded people who Kade didn't have to snarl at. But they were just that: dreams. Dying young was always more likely. Dying young was *simple*. A full stop to the world's messiest run-on sentence. Marriage sounded...complicated. A beautiful mess that Kade would flee from the first time it got hard.

"It's not *you*," he said finally. "It's my giant self-destruct button. It's the Renfield curse of snarling at people and burning down everything good we get. I *want* to keep you, of course I want to keep you. I want... I want all the time I can get with you. I want to be with you so long we watch the sun burn out."

"Oh," Theo said, softer this time. Still holding the vase shards. Still blocking the damn door so Kade couldn't run away like a coward. His face was so unbearably tender Kade couldn't bring himself to look at it.

Kade hoisted the vacuum higher, relieved he had something in his hands. "Hey. After this, let's do something that has nothing to do with our inevitable doom."

Theo's unbearably tender gaze became more manageable. "Watch a TV show we only kind of like so it won't be corrupted ten years from now by thinking, *oh, that's the show I watched when I was waiting for my dad to show up and try to make me kill my boyfriend?*"

"You got it."

Theo hesitated. "Tomorrow? I want—"

Then he froze, his head cocked. Listening for danger, Kade realized with a dull thud of panic. He'd been doing it more often this week.

Kade swallowed. "What's up?"

Theo didn't say anything for a moment. His jaw flexed uneasily. Then he straightened with an unconvincing smile that did nothing for Kade's nerves.

"Probably nothing," Theo said. He cleared his throat. "Uh, I want to train with Liss today. We're going to try and trigger the transformation."

Kade nodded, doing his best not to picture Theo nine feet tall and spindly, his beautiful face pale and ravaged. The wings were badass, sure. The monstrous form was fun in a grotesque kind of way, if you were watching it on-screen and not having it fly at you. But Hawthorn and Victor had been unrecognizable. Kade didn't want Theo to be unrecognizable to him, even for a minute.

"Makes sense," he said. "We'll watch some mindless TV tomorrow."

His toes twitched in his shoes, fingers drumming on the vacuum handle. When Theo felt helpless, his first urge was to throw himself into something productive. When Kade felt helpless, his first urge was to growl at someone and then go and break something. Ideally himself. If Theo left him alone, he was going to do something stupid.

Theo hefted the vase shards. "I'm gonna throw these out."

"Yeah," Kade said. He shook the vacuum. "I'm gonna—"

"I can do that."

Kade shook his head. "I got it."

Theo paused. Wrestling against his programming, trying not to get frustrated. Kade kept his face unjudging and open, a silent version of what he'd told Theo that day in the woods: *I'm not saying you can't do it. I'm helping because I want to help.*

"Alright," Theo said finally, only a little strained. "Thanks."

Kade was proud of Theo for battling his demons, and he tried to focus on that as he watched Theo head down the hall with his hands full of vase shards. But Kade's own demons were closing in, and they were ravenous.

. . .

The Sloan liquor cabinet was tucked away in the corner of the kitchen. Kade had never stolen from it before. He didn't count that time he stole a bottle of vodka from Felicity's house party, since it was from the drinks table, not the cabinet. Even when Felicity let him roam around the house unattended—which took several hangouts—he never stole from the cabinet. Not even the minibar-sized bottles the Sloans had kept from motels.

But the time had come. Kade was honestly surprised it took him this long. Drinking had lost its luster since he got a life. Homework and friends and a boyfriend, not to mention classes he actually went to. Still, he'd been idly planning to get drunk alone in the woods for weeks. Theo assured Kade he could drink around him, but something about it set Kade's teeth on edge. He didn't want Theo to judge how fast he drank. Some people drank for fun; Kade drank for the same reasons he threw himself into fights: because he wanted to destroy something.

"Whatcha doing?" said a voice from the doorway.

Kade banged his head on the liquor cabinet and swore. He'd been leaning in to grab something from the back, rearranging the other bottles so it looked like nothing was missing.

"Jesus Christ," Kade said, turning around to see Felicity leaning against the kitchen counter, chewing gum. "Don't you dare put chocolate in my good jacket again. I had to replace the lining."

Felicity shrugged and sat down, examining the bottles with him. "You haven't asked for this for a while."

Kade waggled the whiskey he was holding. "Maybe I got really good at stealing."

"I'm not my mom, dumbass. I actually keep track of what's in here." She grinned, sticking her gum under the kitchen counter and ignoring his look of disgust. Then she grabbed the whiskey from Kade's hand and cracked the lid. "I have an hour before I'm kicking Theo's ass. He wants to go for a run first. Want to get smashed?"

Kade thought about pointing out the obvious danger in fighting a vampire while wasted. Then he thought about how he never actually *enjoyed* drinking, not like everybody else seemed to. It felt bad from the very beginning. But a wonderful kind of bad, like pressing on a bruise.

Felicity pressed on her bruises all the time. Kade watched her feel them when she was bored during class. He watched her now, tipping the bottle against her mouth before he'd even had a chance to agree.

She held out the bottle.

Kade took it.

"I don't get you," he said when he resurfaced. "I thought I would, once we were friends. But I still don't."

"Good," Felicity said. She smiled, and at first Kade

thought she was genuinely flattered. Then her smile slipped, and she tugged on the new bangs she'd cut when her modeling agency fired her from her latest gig. She only did that when she was trying to hide her hurt.

"So what caused this?" Felicity asked, gesturing at Kade sitting next to her on the kitchen floor with the bottle.

"Other than my inevitable doom? Shit, Liss, I don't know."

"You didn't break into my liquor cabinet yesterday. You were doomed then." Felicity nudged him.

Kade pushed her away halfheartedly. The back of his head was itching again.

"It's been waiting for me all my life," he admitted. "I've felt it. Shadows behind me. Breath on my neck. Now it's finally here. And I can't do anything to stop it."

He lifted the bottle. "I don't know. It's this or break something, and I don't think your mom would appreciate it if I started smashing her stuff."

Felicity was silent for a long time. She took a deep breath, and for a moment Kade thought she was going to say something profound.

"I'm going to grab my favorite knife," she said instead. "If we're getting one-on-one time, we need a knifey fingers rematch."

"Sounds like a great idea," Kade deadpanned. He didn't even remember how their last match ended, only that he'd woken up to Theo healing his torn fingers with a worried look that made Kade want to shut himself in his room and never come out.

Felicity handed him the bottle. He watched her leave, dread still curling in his gut. He took another swallow. That fake ease was spreading through him, blunting all his jagged edges. Maybe if he drank enough, he could finally convince himself what Theo and Sundance had been telling him all year: that he wasn't doomed. That everything was going to be okay.

After a few more swallows, he was even convinced it could work.

Then the screaming started.

THEO WAS STILL BERATING himself when he slowed to a normal pace on Felicity's driveway, picking twigs out of his hair. They didn't have *time* for him to sprint out his feelings. He needed to train. To figure out how to take on Victor. To connect with the monster inside of him and coax it out. Otherwise, he was useless. Victor would take him down just as easily as last time.

He reached for the garage door, trying desperately not to think of Victor shoving him into the ceiling. His gaze turning hard and merciless, so devoid of affection that Theo was *sure* he'd seen before. Back when Theo was obedient. The affection you'd give a dog, as long as it behaved.

Then the screaming started. Not the usual battle bellows Felicity let out when she was training—these were too desperate, too angry. Felicity was in *trouble*.

Theo closed his hand too hard around the garage door handle, warping the metal.

"Shit," Theo barked. He yanked. The handle snapped off. "*Shit!*"

There was a sharp slam behind the garage door, followed by a pained yell.

Theo slammed into the door with all his weight. It dented, the sides folding inwards. One more slam and the metal cracked inwards enough for Theo to shove inside.

Felicity was picking herself up off the concrete. She bent to grab two axes from the rack she'd just been thrown into, baring her teeth in a ghoulish grin.

Victor watched her from the other side of the garage with an amused smile. He was in his human form, wearing the same dress shirt and slacks combination that up until recently, Theo had seen every day of his life. He looked at Theo calmly, as if Theo had walked downstairs for breakfast.

"I always liked her," he said conversationally. "All those sharp edges."

Felicity screeched, "DIE YOU UNDEAD SON OF SHITSUCKING BITCH!"

She lobbed the axes. Victor batted them away, sending them clattering into the walls.

"See?" Victor said. "It comes so *naturally* for her."

The hallway door slammed open. Kade stumbled to a stop, panting. An open bottle of whiskey dangled from his hand, a handkerchief stuffed down its neck. The lighter Theo had given him flickered to life in his other hand.

"Ah," said Victor.

Kade lit the Molotov cocktail and tossed it. Theo streaked across the garage, shielding Felicity with his body as it exploded and scattered flames and weaponry. He cried out, glass and heat scoring his scalp.

"Shit," Kade called. "Sorry, sunshine!"

Felicity let out a terrified giggle. She reached for the crossbow that had fallen next to her on the concrete.

Theo whirled. The scent of burning hair made his eyes water but he could see Victor clearly through the flames: he was frowning, patting out a fire on his lapel. His jaw flexed, and Theo felt the all-encompassing fear of a young child knowing their parent was unhappy with them.

"Alright," Victor said tensely. "That's enough now. I have to talk to my son."

He cracked his neck. Then his shoulders. His legs snapped and lengthened. His skin went pale. A pair of wings exploded from his back.

Beverly burst from the hallway door, a sheer white dressing gown swishing around her ankles. There was a millisecond where she gaped in horror at the vampire mid-transformation in the middle of her burning garage. Then she steeled her expression.

"Mom," Felicity yelled. "Catch!"

She threw a crossbow. Beverly caught it with ease, leveling it at Victor's spindly chest.

Victor's wings flared out. They skimmed the ceiling, tall and spiky and horrible, and Theo was overcome with a wave of loathing: *this* was what he was trying to become. His dad would be so proud. Vicious in every jagged claw and razor fang.

Victor streaked toward Theo, locked his arms around him, and lifted him away from Felicity. Theo struggled, but Victor's grip was unbreakable as he blurred toward the destroyed garage door.

Kade yelled his name. Theo turned, catching a glimpse of Felicity scrounging for an ax, and Beverly stubbornly aiming her crossbow, and Kade patting out a flame from his jacket, his eyes huge and gray as he watched helplessly.

Theo managed one last thought as he stared at the burning garage: *thank god Dad isn't here for him.*

The dented garage door snapped off its hinges.

Victor carried Theo off into the night.

Wind ripped past them, cooling Theo's sizzling scalp. His curls were probably regrowing as they flew, he thought with a seething hatred. His dad's curls were gone now, but they'd be there the second he came back to human form.

Victor stole the spell book from Theo's pocket. "Thank you. I was looking for that."

Theo kicked viciously and uselessly at his inhumanly long legs.

"Still can't transform, hmm?" Victor mused as he carried Theo higher. "Disappointing."

Theo told himself not to react. That this wasn't the man who taught him how to dribble a ball and change a tire and eviscerate someone with a sharp smile and a cold comment. But the shame flooded in anyway, crowding out everything that tried to remind him of Victor smashing him into the floorboards. He wanted to apologize. To beg for mercy. Prove he was still a good son.

He unsheathed his fangs and dug them into Victor's bony shoulder.

Victor laughed, joyous. "See? You still have potential."

They were up so high now, flying over the forest. Toward their old house.

"You know," Victor continued, voice surprisingly neat around his fangs. "I was like you, a long time ago. Caught between who I was and who I needed to be. My maker helped me shed my old self. Make room for the new."

Theo blinked back wind-stung tears and tried to think of a retort. Something Kade would say, brutal and biting. One of Felicity's blunt, snappy comebacks. Aaron's dry, unaffected insults.

"Screw you," Theo hissed.

Victor dug his nails into Theo's arms. "You'll still

have to kill him, you know. If you refuse I'll just make you."

"I'd rather die."

Victor laughed. "Too late for that."

He was slowing down, the forest becoming clearer below them. Victor squeezed Theo tighter. For a dizzying second Theo remembered being five years old, his dad holding him over the pool and promising he wouldn't drop him.

Then, of course, he had. *You have to learn how to swim somehow*, he'd told Theo afterwards, prying his tiny fingers off the edge of the pool. *Into the deep you go.*

"You were made for this," Victor continued.

"Then you made me wrong." Theo bared his teeth, wet with his father's black blood. "I'm not what you wanted."

Victor gazed down at him. His mouth curled into a strange, almost proud smile.

He slowed. They weren't over the house, Theo realized. They were right beside it. The lake waited below them, dark and still. His stomach gave a sickening lurch. Moonlight, pale wings, the lake looming below—they'd done this before.

Victor sunk his claws into Theo's side, dragging out huge chunks of flesh. Theo cried out, almost missing Victor's next words, spoken softly into Theo's ear.

"Give me time," Victor whispered.

Then he let go.

Theo plummeted. He tried to concentrate, to fly out

of danger, but he couldn't focus on anything but the agony. The water was rushing up at him, inevitable, and for a sickening feeling Theo caught the edges of that doomed feeling Kade kept mentioning, *everything has already happened and it is going to happen again*—

He slammed into the lake. It surrounded him, welcoming him back. Dragging him down and down into the depths, until he looked up and the moon was barely a speck.

He kicked. The movement jarred his eviscerated side so badly he had to stop. He stared up at the blurry moonlight in blind panic. He'd never make it in time. Kade wasn't here to pull him out. He was going to drown down here again—

He stopped, blinking through the blackened water.

Dead boys didn't drown. He could wait as long as he liked.

So he waited until his wound numbed enough for him to swim. Every second was torture, the water pressing tighter and tighter around him, growing weaker as black blood pulsed out of his side.

His sneakers touched the bottom of the lake.

Theo shuddered and started swimming.

The moon was huge and bright when he broke the surface. Theo stared at it, gulping useless air. It was like being in a coffin, down there. He had joked to Kade a few times that he was glad he didn't sleep, because he'd have nightmares about the lake. The endlessness, the suffocating dark. Knowing he'd never make it back to the surface. That he was going to die down there, cold and alone.

A faint bark made him look up.

Kade stood at the edge of the forest, frozen in shock. Sparky was at his side with her ears pointed up.

They both moved at once, Kade not bothering to pull his good boots off before he stumbled into the water. Sparky bounded after him, still barking.

"Here," Kade yelled. "He's here, we got him!"

Theo slumped with relief. For a second he just floated there, watching Kade wade deeper and deeper. Then he got a hold of himself.

"I'm fine," he croaked, starting up a flimsy breast-stroke. "You can go back, I'm fine."

But Kade kept coming. By the time Theo reached him, he was doggy-paddling with his head barely above the surface. Sparky had already reached him by then, licking Theo's face and making the swim harder.

"I know," Theo kept telling her. "You heard me, huh? Thanks for coming."

Kade pulled at Theo's wet shirt, eyes widening when he saw the deep wound under the water. "Shit! That's a lot of blood."

"He took the spell book," Theo said.

"Bloody hell." Kade spat out a mouthful of water. "Worry later. Come on, let's get you back on dry land."

He stuck by Theo's side for the whole stilted, awkward swim. The others had reached the shore by then: Felicity with a dagger in each hand, glancing around the forest like she wanted a rematch. Beverly Sloan watching with a severe expression, her gauzy dressing gown streaked with burns. And Skeeter Bass in a ski mask, pulling it up to chew her nails.

"I'm sorry," she blurted as Theo and Kade crawled out of the lake with Sparky behind them, shaking her fur out. "I was coming but you said no one should know I'm there and it sounded bad and I don't know how to fight and I don't want to get in the way—"

"It's fine," Theo said, trying to muster the energy to get up from his hands and knees. "Everyone okay?"

"We're good," Felicity said, still scanning the tree line. "Training arena's less fine. Holy shit, did he *gut* you?"

Theo grimaced. The hole in his side was dripping black blood into the dirt. It was getting harder to think, to move, to do anything but sit there in the muddy dirt, keeping his arms underneath him.

Kade pulled at his sodden shirt, dragging him up.

"What is it?" Theo asked hazily as Kade turned him around. "You hurt?"

"Nope, that's you, genius." Kade held out his wrist. "Come on, emergency dinner time."

Theo swayed on the spot. He looked at the others self-consciously.

"Ignore them," Kade told him. "Just eat."

He held his wrist to Theo's lips. They parted instinctually, and Theo sunk his teeth in. Trying to forget about the lake behind him. About his father's threatening words and the lost spell book. About Sparky whining, Skeeter still apologizing, Felicity cursing, Beverly Sloan saying nothing as usual. Losing himself in Kade, his sweet blood, his gloved hand tracing soothing circles in Theo's healing scalp.

CHAPTER
TEN

"WHERE'S THEO?"

Kade stiffened, caught off guard by Aaron's sudden appearance at their cafeteria table. Thankfully Felicity was already on top of it.

"He's taking a shit," she said with an acidic glare.

Aaron looked like he wanted to remind her that vampires were physically unable to shit, and was cursing the spell that wouldn't let him say it without choking to death on his own splintered organs. He also looked like he wanted to pass out right there on the linoleum. Even his eyebags had eyebags.

"He looked sick," he said instead. "Thought he might've gone home."

"He's fine," Felicity insisted, scratching her burn bandages under her T-shirt. "He's doing *great*. Thanks for checking in."

Aaron looked reluctantly at Kade. Kade bent low

over his meatloaf, wishing Aaron didn't still make him feel like crap. At least it was a different kind of crap nowadays: less loathing and more...squirming, uncomfortable pity.

Aaron didn't want to be in this story either. Last year he had friends, popularity, both parents, both *hands*. He had good hair and good grades and was the second-best player on the basketball team. Now what did he have? His grieving mom and a mission. An ex-best friend and an ex-girlfriend who avoided him in the halls. Kade knew intimately what it felt like to keep walking down a path you never wanted because it was the only one you could see in front of you.

He hated that he could relate to the guy. But he couldn't help it. Aaron just looked so *pathetic*. Gone were the days of cool, aloof Aaron Fletcher, ruling the school with two expressions: bored or smug. Now, anytime he wasn't actively pissed off he looked like he was going to collapse or cry, possibly both at once.

Kade sighed, digging a ripped piece of workbook paper out of his pocket. "Hey Fletcher. You seen any of these?"

He showed him the sketches, ignoring Felicity's warning stare. They weren't anywhere near as detailed as the sketches in the spell book, but they were the best Kade could do when Milly asked for a recreation: a flowy dress, a jagged spear, a flower with pink, diamond-shaped flowers and veins down the middle.

"Kade," Felicity hissed.

"What? We're on the same side. Even if he's a shit." Kade waved the page, inviting him to look but not touch. "Anything?"

Aaron frowned. He bent over the page, looking up at Kade warily. Like he half-expected him to slap him in the face.

"I don't," he started. Then he looked at the flower, and something flickered over his face: confusion going deeper, before arriving at a realization. He smothered it as soon as it came, his face falling into that haughty mask that Kade loathed.

"Nope," he said easily. Then he turned.

"*Hey*," Felicity barked. She scraped her chair back as she stood, shoved in front of him, and stabbed a finger in his face. "I saw that. You can't say shit, but you can *help*. Okay? You *can*. I think you're a lost cause, but you always did love proving me wrong. Are you gonna?"

Her voice shook on the last word. Kade had never heard her voice do that, except at the end of *Spider-Man 3*, when Harry sacrifices himself to save Peter after trying to kill him for the whole movie. Theo had given him a look that clearly meant *if you laugh at her right now she will kill you*, so Kade had wisely shut up.

Aaron's throat worked. "Liss," he said, like an apology.

Felicity's face was already twisting up in disgust. "You were always going to pick them. They treat you like shit, and you still—"

She sat back down with a growl, scratching the burn

bandage on her arm. She mostly didn't let Theo heal the wounds she got during training, no matter how much her mom or Theo or even Kade pushed her toward it. Theo was constantly healing Kade: bite marks and stray bruises and puncture wounds from pricking his finger during sewing. It felt nice, being taken care of. Weird, but nice. Still, Kade completely understood why she didn't let Theo fix it. Why she kept scratching at her wounds, making them heal wrong. Sometimes you wanted to keep the hurt.

"Whatever," she said, grabbing the paper from Kade's hand and stuffing it in her pocket. "Go tell your mommy what you saw and leave us alone already."

Aaron curled his lip. For a second Kade thought he was going to grace them with one of his trademark sneers. Then Aaron ducked his head, and Kade realized that the sneer was still happening, it was just reaching inwards.

"Sucks about Delilah," he muttered.

Felicity paused, still staring determinedly at her tray of nearly demolished meatloaf. "Emmerson? Why, what happened?"

But Aaron was already walking away.

Felicity watched him, eyes narrowed. "The hell was that?"

"No idea," Kade said, unease churning in his gut. He took out a biro from his pocket, spinning it anxiously. "Are you okay?"

"I'm *great*," Felicity snapped, digging her phone out

of her pocket. "I'm awesome. Unlike Delilah Emmerson, who is... oh, shit."

"What?" Kade leaned in, but Felicity was already leaning his way to show him the texts she'd received this morning: Delilah Emmerson was missing. Nobody had seen her since the night before when she went for a run in the woods.

"Shit," Kade whispered, spinning the biro so fast it almost spun out of his hand. "Did we miss something in the spell book? Maybe the ritual *does* need sacrifices."

"Yeah, or maybe he just wants more vamps to wreak vengeance on the town." Felicity shoved her phone in her pocket and looked up, scanning the cafeteria and letting out a hiss of victory. "Sighted."

"What?"

Felicity nodded up at the cafeteria line. Kade turned, expecting to see Theo back from his squirrely snack break.

Delilah Emmerson's sibling was loading rice onto their cafeteria tray, their shoulders hunched. Where Delilah was outgoing—a class president full of unfulfilled campaign promises—Ryan Emmerson ran under the radar. Kade only noticed them because of their black nail polish and baggy denim jacket, which was covered in pins of obscure bands and quotes and assorted flags. They'd only started dressing like that last year, so their fashion wasn't yet fully realized. But it was earnest and more interesting than ninety-five percent of the town population.

Felicity raised her bandaged arm. "RYAN!"

Ryan jerked, whirling around so fast their apple almost toppled off their tray. Kade waved and tried to look nonthreatening, for once. He knew what it was like to be on red alert every time someone called your name.

Felicity yelled, "Come pop a squat over here."

Ryan glanced over at their usual table, where a group of alternatively dressed teens were passing around volumes of manga.

Felicity yelled louder. "Ryan! Squat!"

Ryan hesitated. But Felicity Sloan still had sway at this school, even if it had corroded in the last few months. They headed toward the table.

Kade leaned over. "Are we sure this is a good idea?"

"All my ideas are good ideas."

Kade made a face.

Felicity kicked him under the table. "What if the Emmersons have some shit hidden away, too? What if Vicky's taking people from hunting families? What if—? Oop, time to be cool."

Felicity dragged out a chair between her and Kade, patting the dented plastic.

"There you go," she said as Ryan sat down. She reached over and flicked one of their newer pins. "Cute. No idea where you got that in Lock."

Ryan looked down at the pin she'd flicked. It was a tiny row of flags: the bisexual flag, the trans flag, the LGBT+ flag, and another flag that Kade didn't recognize, gray and white and purple.

"Ordered it online," they mumbled. "Am I being hazed?"

"If that makes it easier to explain," Felicity said. "Yes."

Kade gave her a sideways look. Felicity grabbed his biro, flipping it easily between her fingers.

"Sucks about your sister," she said. "I hope they find her."

Ryan stared at the spinning biro. "Thanks," they said slowly.

"I just wanted to let you know we're rooting for her," Felicity continued.

"Thanks," Ryan repeated. Their eyes flickered to Kade nervously.

Kade had caught them looking at him last year. At first he thought it was for the usual reasons people looked at him. Then he noticed Ryan's gaze lingering on Kade's shirts or his earrings or his eyeliner. Picking up fashion tips. But also, Kade suspected, taking comfort in the knowledge that they weren't the only weirdo in town.

There wasn't any comfort in their face now. But there was a shred of hope. Like they wanted to believe the rumors weren't entirely true. That they weren't being hazed, there was something different going on here, something strange and misunderstood.

Felicity looked over at Kade expectantly.

Kade looked back at her just as expectantly. She was the one from the hunting family, she was supposed to lead the questions. But Felicity just kept staring. She'd picked up on the hope emanating from Ryan, who had averted their eyes down to their tray.

Kade sighed. "Okay. This is going to sound weird, but I promise we're not hazing you. Did your family have any...Lock-related stuff they keep hidden?"

Ryan frowned. "Lock-related stuff?"

"Yeah. Like, maybe a spear. Or a dress. Or some secret flower patch that only blooms one week a year?"

The hope in Ryan's face was waning fast.

Felicity cut in. "What about weird family history shit? Maybe something your grandparents couldn't tell you about. Old photos of ax-wielding ancestors. Saying you were important. Defending the town. Did anyone make you train with weapons and then get really weird and threatening if you tried to tell people?"

Ryan stared at her. It was a bewildered silence, but it wasn't *just* bewildered, their face lurching between confusion and deep horror.

"They said—" Ryan stopped, wetting their lips. They tugged their baggy denim jacket closer, knuckles scraping the endless pins. "Grandpa—Dad's dad—he was kind of weird. Dad doesn't like talking about it. There was a lot of weapons training. Dad said Grandpa was some kind of doomsday prepper. Said we had to be ready."

"For what?" Felicity asked.

Ryan shrugged. "Never told him. It really annoyed Dad. Before he went to college they tried to get him in on the secret. Well, *Grandpa* did, Grandma didn't want to. And Dad said no. Said he didn't want anything to do with it. I think Grandpa was really upset about it. He really believed..." They trailed off, face full of fear and wild hope. "Does this have something to do with Delilah?"

Kade met Felicity's eyes. This was as good as a confirmation: the Emmersons had something Victor wanted.

Felicity flicked her dyed hair out of her face. "Do you do a lot of things alone, Ryan?"

"I guess?"

"Maybe stop that for now."

Kade waited for Felicity to smile. That teasing smile she always did, sharp and mildly infuriating, letting you know she was always one step ahead. But she didn't smile. She just sat there, staring, the biro spinning expertly between her practiced fingers.

"Why?" Ryan whispered.

Kade took over. They wanted to warn Ryan, not freak them out. Or worse, send them scurrying back to their table full of new weird gossip that would make people even more suspicious.

"Just to be safe," he told them. "Liss—"

He broke off as something slammed hard into the side of Kade's chair, sending him sprawling.

He hit the floor with a grunt, pain exploding up his arm. That snarling dog inside him woke up, straining at its leash as he looked into the stupid grinning face of Finn Harley.

"Heard you were bothering a grieving classmate," Finn said. "Pretty rude, Renfield."

"They're not grieving," Felicity pointed out, the biro stilling in her hand. "Delilah's *missing*, jackass. Not dead. Get your facts straight."

Theo had told him not to engage. *Don't let him know we're onto him.* But the guy had just knocked Kade out of his chair. He couldn't *not* react. Maybe it was part of Finn's plan or maybe he was just being an asshole, giddy with the power he was primed to receive, but Kade couldn't *not* react to this shit.

Finn laughed. "Gonna growl at me, Monster? Huh?"

Then he barked.

Kade closed his eyes, trying to remember Aunt Sundance's voice telling him not to give in. Theo's annoyed admonishments as he healed Kade's bloody knuckles, telling Kade to just limp away or call for backup.

Then Finn barked again. Someone on the other side of the cafeteria joined in.

Kade bared his bloody teeth. Some things were in you so deep. Sometimes you wanted to keep the hurt.

He slammed his boot into Finn's shin. Finn's smile vanished as he skidded onto one knee, the perfect height for Kade to kick him in the face.

Kade did. With gusto.

Finn howled in shock and pain. Kade smashed his boot into his chest, and Finn went sprawling backward.

The cafeteria erupted in barks.

Felicity shouted something. Kade didn't hear it. The blood was too loud in his ears, the barking too intense. He snarled as he climbed on top of Finn, cracking his fists into his cheekbones.

Finn held his arms over his face. He flailed out, a clumsy punch.

Kade laughed, smacking it away. If *this* was really Victor's chosen, he'd picked horribly wrong.

Felicity yelled again. This time Kade heard it: "Not the face! Bone on bone, idiot! Go for the soft parts!"

Kade punched him in the stomach. Finn curled inwards, face blooming red. He gasped airlessly.

Kade reared back to punch him again.

Then he paused. Ryan was standing a safe distance behind Finn, frozen in place. There was no hope in their eyes anymore. Just fear. Fear that Kade was just as bad as the rumors said—that he was in a cult, that he *led* the cult, that he dug Theo's dad up, that he made Theo's mom disappear, that he was the corrupter of all things good and pure, a wild animal they should put down for the good of the town.

Kade's fist wavered in midair. Part of him wanted to grab them by the hair and snap that it wasn't *him*, okay, why wouldn't anybody *believe* him? The other part of him, louder and infinitely more tempting, wanted to ignore Felicity's advice and keep smashing Finn's face in, no matter what it would do to his precious hinge joints. Theo could heal him later. Better yet, Theo could leave them raw and scabbing, let everybody see what happened when you messed with—

Felicity's strong arms closed around him, twisting his nipples like a maniac.

Kade jerked back. "Liss! Jesus!"

Felicity dropped her face close to his ear, her whisper louder than the barking.

"Save it for later," she hissed.

Finn stared up at him, dazed. His nose was busted, blood running down his chin. Only some of it was Kade's.

Kade went still. Felicity let go of his nipples, and Kade rose stiffly to his feet. His leg still ached where Finn had kicked it.

Finn stumbled up after him, tears in his eyes. "Broke my fugging *nose*," he cried. "You're...I'm gonna..."

"Oh shit," Felicity said as the barking died down. "Guard dog incoming."

Kade looked up just in time to see Theo charge in. He grabbed Finn by his bloodied letterman jacket. His blunt teeth were bared, and Kade had a twisted moment of euphoria, Felicity's words echoing through his head. Guard dogs, both of them. Twin mutts circling the same chain.

"What'd I say?" Theo demanded, shaking Finn hard. "Huh?"

Finn spluttered, blood dripping down his neck.

"*Don't* go near him," Theo spat.

"He attacked me!" Finn wailed.

Ryan spoke up from behind them. "Finn started it."

Kade looked over. Ryan was rigid and small, trying to disappear into their denim. They said nothing else, and scurried back toward their table when they saw Kade looking.

Theo reached up like he was going to touch Kade's face, as if after all this time he still forgot. Then he faltered, dropping his hand to grip Kade's jacket instead. He was staring at Kade's bloody lips.

"I didn't bite him," Kade said.

"I know," Theo replied, his pupils far too big as he stared at Kade's red mouth.

THEO MADE him list his injuries.

"Come on," he said when Kade rolled his eyes. "You can't go to English spitting blood. Just tell me."

Kade twisted his cigarette between his fingers. They were in the disabled bathrooms again, a spot Kade was getting truly attached to. If they made it to graduation, they'd have to have some grand send-off in here. Maybe one last cigarette, their fingers bumping carelessly as they shared it. If they made it to graduation, the ritual would be dead and they'd be able to touch each other. At least, Kade hoped.

"My leg stings," he started. "But that's going away. Tongue hurts, bit the shit out of that. My nipples hurt."

Theo made a face. "Your *nipples*? Did he punch them?"

"No, Liss twisted them. I'm just glad she didn't stab

me with that pen." Kade blew a stream of smoke. "How are you?"

He nodded toward the bandages peeking out from under Theo's shirt.

"I'm fine." Theo took the cigarette out of his hand and stubbed it out on the wall. "Open your mouth."

Kade's breath hitched.

"For your tongue," Theo explained.

"Right. Yeah." Kade opened his mouth wide, jaw clicking with effort. He figured Theo would tell him to cope with it, a bitten tongue wasn't that big of a deal. But now Theo was sliding his fingers over Kade's tongue, his touch unbearably gentle even as it seared him.

Kade let out a pained noise.

"I know," Theo said, grimacing. "Almost done."

Kade's eyes watered. The pain ebbed, first the throb of the bite and then the burn Theo had created. There was a millisecond when Theo's fingers were solid and cool against his tongue, and Kade's heart leapt.

Then Theo pulled his fingers out.

"All done," he said, voice high and strange. He cleared his throat, wiping his shiny fingers on his jeans.

Kade shifted on the spot, cheeks burning. Was now a good time to bring up the secret sex-related Google searches he'd done while Theo was making dinner? It was, Kade was embarrassed to discover, very possible. It was just...less dignified than Kade hoped. Less *intimate*. And they still couldn't kiss. Which Kade really, *really* wanted. He just wasn't sure if he was willing to die without having technically-kind-of-sex with Theo because he was holding out for a kiss.

Kade swallowed, gearing himself up to ask. For some reason it was stupidly difficult. He'd *had* sex before, sort of. And he was ninety-five percent sure Theo wanted him, even if Theo had seen him drunk and crying and seething and pathetic too many times to count. But he couldn't make the words come out.

"What'd he say?" Theo asked.

Kade startled. "Huh?"

"Finn," Theo said. He reached into Kade's jeans pocket, pulling out another cigarette and the lighter Theo had gotten him. "Did he say anything weird? Anything we can use?"

Kade swallowed. His cheeks were still red, his tongue still buzzing from Theo's touch. "No. He was just being his regular asshole self."

Theo lit a cigarette. "You're sure?"

"I don't know." Kade held out a hand expectantly.

But Theo put the cigarette back to his mouth and took another drag. "So Finn hit you first?"

Kade waited. When it became clear Theo wasn't going to let this drop, Kade sighed. "No."

"Kade," Theo said, the disappointment in his voice making Kade's insides shrivel. He finally handed the cigarette over.

Kade took it, regret flooding through him in waves. Regret for punching that asshole, for not being able to talk to Theo about what he wanted, for not being able to *have* what he *really* wanted. All he could have was this: a shared cigarette, damp at the tip with Theo's spit.

Kade put it between his lips. "He kicked me. Okay? You know it's harder when they actually *touch* me. Pitbull brain kicks in."

"I know," Theo said. "I just—"

"Well, *I'm* just sick of being Lock's monster. Alright?" Kade took a long, hard drag of the cigarette. His mouth still tasted like blood. Blood and burning.

Theo started to speak. Kade knew what he'd say: they were getting out of here. Kade was going to fashion school and Theo was doing...*something*, he wasn't sure yet, now that he wasn't going to join his parents law firm. Something with plants—gardening. Landscaping. Maybe cooking. Whatever they did, they were doing it far away from Lock.

Kade couldn't stand to hear it again. "We need to raid the Emmerson place," he said, cutting Theo off. "Delilah's missing. She went for a run in the woods, and..."

He trailed off. Theo's face had tightened, his jaw flexing hard enough to crack stone.

"They might have some of the shit he needs," Kade continued. "Or he's turning people and adding them to his vampire army. Even if it's that, we still need to check her house in case she's got a spear hanging in a secret room. Or a dress. Or—"

Theo took the pouch out of his pocket and dug through it, rooting pink petals out of the dirt and holding them over the open toilet.

"Wait," Kade blurted. "What are you doing?"

Theo frowned. "Throwing them out? We have photos. Keeping them feels like I'm just waiting around until he bursts back in to beat the shit out of me again."

Kade watched the petals glint in the dim bathroom light. The idea of watching them vanish down the drain made him choke up in panic. They didn't belong in a sewer, they belonged with them. Taken care of. Cherished.

Since when am I the one getting emotional over plants, Kade wondered.

He stubbed out his cigarette. "Just...give them here first. The pouch, too. Been meaning to look at those bones anyway, I'm pretty sure they're human finger bones."

Theo snorted. But he dropped the petals back into pouch and held it out.

Kade took it. There was a strange moment of vertigo where his vision blurred, and he had to blink hard to clear it. Then he reached into the pouch and dug through the petals for the small, thin bones that had been in his dreams last night, half-remembered and hazy and horrifying—

Kade's vision tunneled. He tipped forward, not even able to enjoy Theo catching him as he—

· · ·

—*falls.*

Theo's hand flashes out, catching Kade by the back of his coat.

"Goddamned root," Kade complains. He straightens, waiting for the inevitable admonishment. But Theo simply stands there, hand tight in Kade's coat, standing closer than Kade remembered. He is beautiful, even in the darkness. His silhouette makes Kade ache for things they can never have.

He swallows, stepping back. "Thank you. Again."

Theo lets go of his coat, expression unreadable. He starts walking once more, and Kade follows. It is the third time he has tripped in these dark woods tonight. Each time, Theo catches him and pulls him back up. By the coat, of course. They have not been able to touch each other without painful consequences for almost a year.

"We could kill ourselves," Kade suggests.

Theo shoots him an exasperated look.

"What?" Kade asks. "It would fix it. He would have no lock, no key. We're his only chance at seeing her again and razing the town."

"We're not dying," Theo insists. "We're undoing this. We will find a way out of this curse he's bound us to, and then we will live. Far away from here."

Kade sighs. "Theo."

"We will *undo this," Theo says over him. "I've spoken to the hunter's spellcaster. She says there is something we can do."*

Kade's stomach twists. He can't afford to let himself hope. He'd learned long ago that was a luxury meant for the lucky. Kade has never been lucky as long as he lived. He thought he might've been, when he met Theo. Then that turned into yet another doomed story.

"Is this why you brought me into the woods so late?"

"No," Theo replies.

"Then why?"

"Because of this." Theo lets him go and reaches into his pocket. When he brings it back out, his fingers are curled around something small and pink.

Kade cannot hold back a smile. "Already?"

"Just in time," Theo says softly.

His hand—

—opened.

Kade groaned, squinting in the bright light of the nurse's office.

Theo loomed over him, those beautiful brown eyes wide with concern. Kade remembered the day of Victor's funeral, lying on the grass after Theo dragged him out of the car Kade had wrecked.

"We have to stop meeting like this," Kade slurred.

Theo frowned. "What?"

Kade shook his head, making the plastic sheets under him crackle. He so rarely got to lie down on the cot, Kade mused as he waited for his head to stop spinning. Usually, Nurse Telfar threw a bandage and some aspirin at him and told him to stop being a stain on the student population.

Kade squeezed his eyes shut against the aching

lights. The vision was already fading, like trying to remember a dream upon waking. No matter how much he tried to argue with his own visions—*they're my memories, a previous version of me but they're MINE, quit taking them*—they dissolved anyway.

Nurse Telfar appeared over Theo's shoulder, glaring under those magnificent bushy eyebrows. "Is he on something? I have to report him if he is."

"He's not on anything," Theo said defensively.

Nurse Telfar glowered at him. She was well loved by the majority of the student body. She let girls curl up on the cot while they waited for the pain pills to kick to dull their cramps. She even turned out the light for one student who got chronic migraines. But like most of the town, she had little sympathy for Kade. He'd stumbled in on the third day of freshman year with a black eye and swollen knuckles. She'd taken one look at him— ripped jeans, a dozen earrings, smudged eyeliner, a shirt with a word on it that would soon get him suspended— and said, *I hope you haven't been causing trouble.*

"I'll take him home," Theo assured her. He slid a hand under the small of Kade's back, easing him up. "Come on."

Kade hummed, sagging forward. That vision had taken more out of him than usual. His head flopped onto Theo's shoulder.

Theo jerked away. "Careful."

Kade peeled his eyes open. He'd come dangerously close to shoving his forehead into Theo's exposed neck.

The nurse turned away, grumbling as she tidied the cot where Kade had been lying. Straightening the sheets. Brushing the pillows free of Kade's filth.

Kade waited until the door closed behind them, then turned to Theo. "I *had* it. I *knew* where those flowers were, and then it was gone. Where the hell are we even supposed to *look*?"

"No idea," Theo said, his arm a wonderful clamp around Kade's waist. "But I know who might."

THEO KNOCKED EIGHTEEN TIMES.

Nobody answered.

"Maybe he's not home," Kade whispered.

"He's home, I can hear him moving around," Theo told him. He cocked his head, listening to the footsteps stop. Russel would be checking the peephole.

"Theo?" Russel said finally. "Is that you? Isn't it a school day?"

"I have a gardening question," Theo replied. "It's urgent."

He waited, heart in his throat. Russel used to tell Theo that he could call anytime. He hadn't said that since Theo hoisted him up in the air over Victor's empty grave, but Theo hoped it was still true.

There was a long pause. Theo swallowed. He should've called him to apologize, like Sundance had suggested. He'd meant to. He just got so consumed by school and his drop from popularity and his parents' monstrous betrayal and his new boyfriend. Apologizing to Russel had fallen by the wayside.

Kade touched his sleeve. "Maybe we should come back later."

"Wait," Theo said. "Just...one second."

The door cracked open.

"Hi," Theo said. "Look, I'm really sorry—"

He stopped. The smell of dried blood washed over him.

"Oh shit," Kade muttered.

The left side of Russel's face was swathed in bandages. The material was dark, due for changing. A cut peeked out along his chin. It was a slash wound. A *claw* wound, if you were being picky about it.

Russel gave them a cautious nod.

"Boys," he said. "What can I do for you?"

"Russel," Theo said. "You're...what *happened?*"

Russel shifted guiltily in the doorway. "What? Nothing happened."

The scent of blood wafting from him said otherwise. Theo held his breath.

Russel reached up like he was going to touch the bandages, then dropped his hand hastily. Like he didn't want to draw attention to them. Like they weren't taking up half of his face, blocking his left eye and *still* not covering all the wounds.

"Russel," Theo repeated. "Seriously. What happened?"

Russel cleared his throat. "I fell."

"Doesn't look much like a fall."

"Well, shows what you know." Russel made a face like it physically pained him to be mean to Theo, which was...nice. Then he made another face, pained, because making faces had to hurt with all those claw marks. "Can I help you? I'm busy."

He was *definitely* tangled up in some hunter stuff, Theo decided. Skeeter's savior hadn't been a random guy with an ax. Russel wouldn't treat Theo so standoffishly unless he was being fed some lies from the Fletchers. Even after Theo dangled him in the air in front of Victor's empty grave, he'd still tried to understand. Tried to *help*.

"Right. I won't take up much of your time." Theo dug the flower petals out from his pocket. "Have you seen these before?"

Russel's guarded expression flickered to pure confusion. "You...ditched school. To ask about flowers?"

"Are we still playing into this?" Kade continued. "We know you're involved, dude. And we're not your enemies, so stop glaring at Theo."

"I don't know what you're talking about," Russel said. "And—and even if I did, I wouldn't say anything. I *can't* say anything."

Kade groaned. "Jesus, not you too. What's so appealing about a spell that kills you if you snitch? How did they rope you into that? Was this before you attacked Vicky or after?"

"*Vicky?*" Theo muttered.

Kade sighed. "Felicity thought we should have a less threatening name for your deadly vampire dad."

Russel started to close the door. Theo shoved his leg in the way. Russel winced and held the door open. As if one flimsy door could harm Theo Fairgood. His dad had torn a chunk out of his side a few days ago and he was walking it off.

"You could really slam it," Kade suggested. "It wouldn't hurt. Except emotionally."

"I don't know how you got roped into this," Theo told Russel. "But we're not the bad guys, Russel. We're trying to stop the bad guys. The Fletchers don't trust vampires. But I'm not just a vampire, I'm *me*. And you *know* me. I know I scared you, back at...at the grave. I thought you hurt my dad. My mom tricked me into believing it. I never should've, but I did. I guess after Hawthorn tried to kill me it wasn't that big of a leap."

"*What?*" Russel said, appalled.

Theo talked over him. "But here's what we know. Victor needs three things—not including us—to complete the ritual. One of them is these flowers. If we destroy them, he can't complete the ritual. So if you know where they are, you *have* to tell us. Or...or tell Mrs. Sloan, and she'll do it. Hell, tell the Fletchers! I don't care who does it, just that it gets done."

Russel frowned at the petals. Then he hissed in pain, the frown pulling hard at the injuries.

Theo grimaced in sympathy. "Shit. Want me to heal you?"

Russel gave him a bewildered look. "Excuse me?"

"He can heal your face," Kade said.

Russel's expression only got more bewildered.

Kade sighed. "Did they not mention it while they were giving you a lowdown of vampire powers? They can heal humans. Otherwise I would've been walking around with bite marks all the time."

Russel hesitated. "What do you need to do?"

"Just touch your face," Theo said. "That's it."

Russel pulled at the end of a bandage. "Do I need to take this off?"

"Not yet," Theo said. He tucked the petals back into the pouch and reached up. Russel watched him cautiously, but didn't move away.

Theo touched Russel's chin and concentrated. The hum was stubborn, as it always was when he healed someone without biting them first. But it vibrated down his fingertips and into Russel's skin until the tear closest to Theo's touch started to seal up.

Russel gasped. After a few more seconds, the scent of blood was contained to the dirty bandages. Russel reached up with shaking hands and unwound the bandages, revealing the left side of his face: sweaty and compressed, but intact.

"*There* we go," Kade muttered.

Theo stood back, waiting. Did he even know anything? He'd seemed genuinely confused by the flowers, staring at the petals in Theo's hand with a troubled expression. Russel took a deep breath.

"That girl," he said tensely. "At the Founder's Day party."

His jaw worked like he desperately wanted to say more but didn't dare. He would know about her body being stolen from the funeral home. Everybody in Lock knew by now.

"She's safe," Theo said. "You saved her."

Russel slumped with relief. "Okay. Alright."

Theo waited as Russel touched his intact face with increasing wonder.

"You should go talk to the Fletchers," he said finally.

Theo sighed. "They won't talk to us."

"Walk around the grounds, then." Russel smiled thinly, a muscle bouncing in his jaw. "I always liked their garden."

Theo opened his mouth to point out that the Fletchers' garden was boring and shorn and colorless, and now it was boring and *overgrown* and colorless. Then he caught Russel's meaningful look.

"Oh," Theo said. "Okay, we'll—"

He froze. He had been mentally cataloging the garden, trying to remember a single spot of color in that big space and coming up with nothing.

Kade turned to him. "What?"

Theo gave Russel a distracted nod and dragged Kade down the stairs by his elbow.

"Remember the greenhouse?" he whispered, leaning in as close to Kade as he dared. "Hidden out the back with the weird glazing so you can't see in?"

Kade's face filled with horrified realization.

"Shit," he whispered.

"Shit," Theo agreed, and ran for the car.

THEO FELT it as they hit Aaron's driveway: a *yank*. Right in the center of his dead chest, hard and urgent.

A startled noise tore out of his chest, not unlike a dog's whine.

Kade looked over. He was clutching the grab handle above the door, his eyes wide. "What is it?"

Theo stomped on the brake. The Lexus skidded to a stop, Kade yelping and almost falling into the windshield despite his death grip on the grab handle.

"Guard dog incoming," Theo said.

Kade frowned. Before he could say anything, Sparky burst out from the trees and raced past them, barking wildly.

Theo pointed. "Look."

Kade swore as he spotted the plume of smoke drifting up from behind the Fletcher house.

Kade snapped his seatbelt off. "Is Victor there?"

Theo concentrated. It was hard to hear anything with Kade so close, his familiar metallic scent and his thundering heartbeat blocking everything else out. Then Kade flung open the car door and the world bled through: Sparky barking. Plastic burning. Blood and ash and dirt. Mrs. Fletcher screaming, Aaron yelling something about gasoline, about crossbows, about Russel's text.

"I'm gonna go with *yes*," Theo said, and raced into the backyard with Kade on his heels.

The greenhouse was on fire. Plastic melted down the blackened wooden struts, dripping onto the burning floor of flowers. They were ash, barely a shred of pink to be seen.

Except for the ones in Victor's hand. Those were bright and vibrant, no matter how many flames Mrs. Fletcher aimed at them with her rapidly weakening flamethrower.

Victor laughed, the noise cracked and raspy as he flew up into a tree.

"Perhaps I'll turn your son," he goaded. "Would you like that, Jan? Would you be a good little hunter and cut off his head?"

Mrs. Fletcher screamed and yanked on the trigger. The flames sputtered and died. She threw the flamethrower at him. He jumped to another branch, the metal crashing harmlessly where he'd been seconds before.

Mrs. Fletcher turned toward the trees, her face blotchy with tears and burns.

"AARON," she yelled.

Aaron stumbled out of the burning greenhouse, his hair singed and his clothes stinking of gasoline, a crossbow in his hand.

Theo squinted. The crossbow wasn't in his hand—it was *attached* to his hand. He had a crossbow harnessed to his stump.

"Crossbow hand," Kade blurted excitedly.

"Later," Theo told him.

Aaron's eyes watered from the smoke as he aimed. A bolt flew from his crossbow. Victor caught it with his free hand, which smoked around the silver before he snapped it in half.

Sparky burst into view, teeth bared as she ran for Victor.

Victor whistled. The noise was sharp and inhuman, making everybody flinch.

"Don't," Theo yelled, heart plummeting.

Sparky's gait stiffened. Her paws twisted over each other as she came to a lurching stop in the smoldering remains of the greenhouse. There was a moment where she went completely still, and Theo thought they might be in the clear. Then she righted herself and kept running. Straight at Mrs. Fletcher.

Theo yelled her name. Sparky ignored him, collided with Mrs. Fletcher, and knocked her into the burning flowers. Mrs. Fletcher let out a frenzied yell, pummeling Sparky's torso with her scabbed fists.

Theo sprinted over and locked his arms around Sparky's torso.

"Quit it," he growled as she struggled. "This isn't you! Come back!"

"Getting away," Kade yelled.

Theo looked over his shoulder, watching helplessly as Victor took off. The flowers glinted in his hand, a bouquet of doom dressed in pretty pink.

Aaron aimed. An arrow streaked through Victor's wing, earning a pained yell but no lost momentum. By the time Aaron reloaded his crossbow hand, Victor had vanished above the trees.

"Shit," Theo spat.

Mrs. Fletcher screamed, reaching up like she was going to dig her thumbs into Sparky's eyes.

Theo yanked Sparky off. She barked, but she was getting quieter by the second. The further Victor got, the less hold he had over her.

"*No*," Mrs. Fletcher yelled. She sat up, paying no attention to the smoldering flowers sticking to her shirt or the sparks climbing her hair. "Goddammit! Useless, you're *useless*!"

She stormed toward them. No crossbow, no flamethrower, just pure rage and burning hair that made Theo think about those pirate stories Kade told him during detention last month about Blackbeard tying smoking fuses into his beard. It did make for a terrifying sight, and Theo dragged Sparky back without thinking.

Mrs. Fletcher had been different since her husband died. No more lipstick, no more PTA meetings. No more stopping in the grocery store to chat to her friends. She got her groceries delivered and talked to no one. The last direct communication Theo had with her was the text barring him from her husband's funeral, and another text a day after he offered to heal Aaron's hand, saying that he wasn't to talk to her son ever again.

Theo tried not to push. He understood her anger. He just didn't want her to point it at him, dark and dripping like the cut on her face.

Kade ran between them, his hands raised. "*We're* useless? We just got here, lady. You let him get the flowers, why did you even *have* them? Just burn them and get them over with!"

Mrs. Fletcher glared at him. "They wouldn't—"

"*Mom*," Aaron said, appalled. He rushed over and patted her hair until it stopped smoking. She shoved him off, holding his crossbow hand so tight Theo wondered if Aaron could feel it. She used to do that when he was a kid, holding Aaron's hand so hard it hurt and snapping at him if he squirmed.

"They wouldn't," Kade repeated. He kicked at a burning clump of flowers, the petals crumbling under the lightest touch of his boot. "What, wouldn't burn? Because these looked pretty burned to me."

"Russel texted them," Theo said. He lowered Sparky to the ground, keeping a hand on her collar just in case.

Kade paused. Then he laughed, the noise strangely eerie over the sound of dying flames and Mrs. Fletcher's ragged breathing.

"You didn't *know*, huh? Didn't know it would be Theo. Didn't know it would be me. Didn't know what he needs for the ritual. You were really in the dark, huh? Generations of trickle-down whispers." Kade's smile twisted, the desperation creeping in as he stepped closer to Mrs. Fletcher. She didn't move back, and the hairs on Theo's neck prickled when he noticed how dark her eyes were. He'd seen Kade get up in people's faces before, but not when they were this angry. Not when they had murder in their blood.

"He has everything he needs but the dress," Kade said in a low voice. "Hell, maybe he already has it! We don't know! What we *do* know is that you had one secret ingredient at the back of your house the whole time, and you only burned it when Victor already had them in his goddamn hand! So don't get mad at us when *you're* the one who screwed the town over."

Mrs. Fletcher jerked forward. Theo almost did the same, only stopping when Aaron held his crossbow hand out and blocked her from going after Kade.

"Mom," Aaron said, ignoring Kade's surprised look. "Let's go."

"This is *my* house," Mrs. Fletcher replied, shaking with rage. Her mouth worked silently, her wet eyes never leaving Kade as she struggled against all the words that wanted to leave her mouth. She couldn't say any of them. None of them except:

"Get the hell out."

Kade groaned. "Stop treating us like we're these big bad monsters you have to defeat! I'm just some teenager trying to make it to twenty, and your husband tried to KILL me because he couldn't be bothered trying other options!"

"Shut your mouth," Mrs. Fletcher whispered.

Kade shoved a middle finger in her face. "You shut *yours!*"

"Kade," Theo tried.

Kade spun on him, burned flowers crumbling to ash under his boots. They smelled so horribly familiar it made Theo's eyes water.

"No, man! Screw your whole 'we need to be nice to her because her husband died.' I'm *glad* he died!"

"Renfield," Aaron said. It wasn't a threat. It was a warning. He still had his arm in front of his mother, stopping her from going after Kade. He was pale and shaky and looked like he would rather be anywhere else but standing between his mom and his ex-situationship, trying to talk them down.

It was getting harder by the second. Mrs. Fletcher was trying to wrestle Aaron's arm away, and Kade wore the same expression as when he was cracking his fists into Finn in the cafeteria: *attack-dog face,* Kade had called it once. *When nothing matters but going for the throat.*

"Your whole family is *awful*," Kade continued, his blunt teeth bared. "You think you're these great big protectors! Newsflash, you're not protecting *shit*. Your husband died choking on his own blood, and you know what, Jan? He deserved every *second* of it."

Mrs. Fletcher let out an anguished cry. At first Theo thought she was still trying to wrench Aaron's arm away so she could launch herself at Kade with her bare hands. But then she shoved the crossbow arm around. The tip grazed Kade's chest—

"NO," Theo yelled. He dropped Sparky and rushed at Mrs. Fletcher, knocking her into the smoldering flowers. He ripped Aaron's arm harness off and was about to throw it into the trees when he noticed Aaron's horrified expression. He was staring at the crossbow harness in Theo's hand.

The *empty* crossbow.

Theo stared at it numbly. Then he turned, hoping with everything in him that he was somehow wrong about the sudden burst of blood in the air.

Kade stood perfectly still, his gray eyes fixed on Theo. A single drop of blood tracked down those chapped lips Theo had spent so long watching as he slept.

Slowly, as if in a dream, Kade reached up and touched the silver bolt sticking out of his chest.

"Yeah," he croaked. "Okay. That's...what I get, I guess."

He sagged forward.

Theo rushed to catch him. Kade's forehead scraped his cheek, the scent of burned skin joining the stench of burned flowers.

"Sorry," Theo blurted. He needed to get Kade somewhere safe. Needed to get him away from Mrs. Fletcher. The burns could wait, the soft skin of Kade's cheek sizzling as Theo hauled him into his arms.

Aaron was yelling, shoving himself in front of his mother. Trying to stop her from another attempt, trying to stop Sparky from lunging at her.

"Call him off," Aaron begged. "Theo! Call him off!"

"Sparky," Theo said. "Stop."

Sparky growled and took a hesitant step back, hackles still up. Then she ran to Kade's side, butting her head anxiously against his leg.

"It's better this way," Mrs. Fletcher argued, eyes wet as she tried to get out from behind her son. "Your father would've—"

"You said not YET," Aaron screamed. He grabbed her arm and started yanking, shooting Theo a disturbed look over his shoulder. For a second Theo thought he was scared of him.

Then Aaron pulled harder at his mom, telling her, "Go, for god's sake!" and Theo realized: Aaron was scared *for* Theo. For him and Kade. Whatever their disagreements, Aaron didn't want to see them butchered in the woods.

Theo lowered Kade into the ashy flowers and lifted his head gently into his lap. The Fletchers' clumsy footsteps were fading, Kade's stuttering heartbeat growing louder with each wet pulse. The arrow had grazed his heart. Theo could hear the blood gushing inside him, filling all the wrong places.

Kade dragged in a wet breath. "Th-think I might've deserved that."

"Shut up," Theo told him. "Just...just keep quiet, I'll handle this."

Kade spasmed with wet coughs. Blood oozed down his chin. "D-did you see his crossbow hand? So cool. I bet he's gonna be so weird about it. I'd *love* a crossbow hand—"

Theo ripped the arrow out of Kade's chest.

Kade let out an agonized cry. Sparky licked his forehead forlornly.

"I know," Theo said, tearing Kade's shirt open. "I know, I'm sorry."

He pressed his hand over the hole. It was the first time he'd touched Kade's bare chest. A burning handprint bloomed against the pale skin. Kade writhed in pain as Theo sealed up the entrance wound.

Sparky whined, dropping her head against Kade's shoulder.

Kade lifted a trembling hand to stroke her head. "G-good dog."

"I'm gonna do your back now," Theo blurted.

Kade caught his sleeve.

"Can't cauterize the inside." Kade smiled shakily, teeth stained red. "Think it might be time, blood boy."

Theo shook his head.

"Come on," Kade croaked. He tweaked Theo's curls, wrapping the biggest one around his finger. "Kill me, sunshine. Then bring me back to you."

"Not yet," Theo whispered.

"Running out of..." Kade started. Then he stopped, choking. Theo didn't know if he was going to say *time* or *blood*.

This wasn't the plan. If Theo turned him now, Kade's last meal would be that cheese sandwich he'd eaten in the Lexus. Kade was supposed to get a last meal with all those disgusting British foods. Theo had been looking up how to make them. Kade was supposed to hug Sundance before it happened, and have a good long sleep, and—

"Burned her paws," Kade mumbled.

"What?"

"Sparky...paw pads..." Kade trailed off with a gurgle. His gray eyes went hazy and unfocused, then dropped shut.

Theo wrenched Kade's head to the side and dug his fangs into Kade's limp neck. Blood filled his mouth, and for the first time Theo didn't lose himself to it. He took a desperate drag and then pulled back. He gnawed his wrist open and brought his wet skin to

Kade's mouth. Black blood dripped past Kade's slack lips.

"Come on," Theo whispered. "Come on, baby. You can do this."

A burned petal landed in Kade's hair. Theo brushed it off, careful not to touch his scalp. Kade wasn't swallowing. Why wasn't he swallowing the blood?

"Always," Kade said again, his beautiful heartbeat thudding slower and slower. "Always knew I was gonna die in these woods. I ever tell you that? First day...I moved here. Went for a walk. 'N I knew, I *knew* it. In my bones..."

He trailed off. His hand slackened on Theo's sleeve, falling into the ashen flowers. Sparky nosed his fingers, whining.

"Kade," Theo whispered. "*Kade!*"

He shook him. It was no use: Kade's gray eyes were blank and unseeing. The black blood rested uselessly on his lips. Theo still couldn't tell if any of it had made it down his throat. His heartbeat was silent.

Kade Renfield was dead.

"ARE YOU READY?"

Kade startles. Theo stares at him, his face grave.

It feels wrong, doing this in the nest of flowers Theo has grown for him. But the hunters asked for a place that had special significance to them, and this was the first place they thought of.

The hunters wait. Several of them stay beyond the clearing, hands on their axes. Only two have ventured into the clearing: the wizened spellcaster, staring wordlessly. And her scarred assistant, her carving knife poised over Kade's thumb. Waiting.

"Sorry," Kade says. "I felt as if I was somewhere else. Yes, I'm...I'm ready. Do it."

The assistant nods. The knife flashes.

Kade bites hard on his lip to muffle his cry. The pain in his mouth is nothing compared to the harsh, unrelenting agony of his severed thumb, gathered quickly into the pouch the hunter holds beneath it.

The assistant shifts the knife to Theo's thumb. The blade flashes again.

Theo lets out a pained grunt as his thumb follows Kade's into the pouch. His eyes flicker black, gaze intent on the blade as the assistant wipes it on her tunic. She hands the pouch over to the spellcaster, who cradles it in her wrinkled hands and starts to whisper.

Theo takes Kade's bleeding thumb, sterilizing and then healing the wound with a touch. Kade grits his teeth as the burn recedes. When Theo lets go, there is a newly healed stump where his thumb was.

"There we go," Theo says, his own thumb still bleeding freely. He reaches into his vest pocket and frowns.

Kade fumbles in his own pocket. "Here. Let me."

Theo lets Kade tie his moth-eaten handkerchief around the wet black stump of Theo's thumb. It soaks through instantly, and Theo touches the embroidered ferns Kade has stitched so carefully over the edges. The pained twist of his mouth pulls sideways into a fond smile. For a second Kade thinks that Theo will say something sweet. Then Theo looks self-consciously at the hunters gathered around them and straightens, the smile fading.

"You're sure this will work?" he asks the assistant.

The assistant does not look at him, cleaning spots of black blood from her fingernails as the spellcaster's chanting grows louder.

Theo gives Kade a weary look.

"Another one we can no longer talk to without risking their vital organs," Kade says. "Lovely."

One of the hunters speaks up over the chanting. "It will work. And then you will go forth and put an end to all of this."

She fixes Theo with a hard look. Kade withholds a sigh.

"I still think we can find another way," Theo starts.

"Theo," Kade says.

But Theo is already shaking his head.

"No," he continues as the chanting rises behind them, more voices joining it. "This is a last resort. I won't let you die."

Kade smiles. His stubborn vampire, trying to craft a happy ending where there is none. He takes a deep breath, spring air flooding his lungs, and looks over to see the spellcaster and her hunters—

—crouched in Felicity's kitchen.

Kade blinked, dazed. The room was a mess of shattered crockery and plaster, a blender cracked in half at his feet.

He was huddled in a corner, a broken mug dripping blood into his hands. He must have taken a bite out of it, Kade realized as he ran his tongue around his mouth, tasting gritty ceramic and something else so tantalizing Kade growled.

"Kade," said Theo.

Kade looked up.

Theo was standing in the doorway, his hands raised in a pacifying gesture. His cheeks were wet with smudgy black tears, his shirt wet with delicious, drying blood.

Not the romantic awakening I was hoping for, Kade thought.

"I was right," he slurred.

Theo frowned. "What?"

"Finger bones," Kade whispered. Then he shoved his fingers against his eyelids, pressing until he saw spots. Until the flowers and flames and blood were gone, the dull throb of his own head rushing in to fill the spaces. He needed to tell Theo what he had seen. But first, he needed to know if his grand plan had worked.

"Everybody's in the living room," Theo said, relief thick in his voice. He was looking at Kade like he was something amazing, not some grubby monster rising from a kitchen he had destroyed.

"Sundance is on her way," Theo continued, wiping his smudgy cheeks clean. "That was...pretty intense. How do you feel?"

Kade tried to find an answer. He felt half awake, one foot in a dream. He felt strange and out of control, the broken mug creaking in his hands. More than anything, he felt like charging up and wrapping Theo in a hug, burying his face in Theo's neck and breathing in until the world made sense.

He took a step forward. Theo's hands twitched at his sides, like he had been thinking the exact same thing.

Felicity's voice echoed in from the hallway. "Can I come in now, or is he still cuckoo for cocoa puffs?"

"One second," Theo called back. He took a cautious

step toward Kade, hands still outstretched. "You have a little..."

He gestured at Kade's cheek, streaked with blood and plaster and burned petals.

"Come and get it then," Kade whispered.

Theo smiled, so full of wild hope that Kade could hardly stand to look.

Please, Kade thought deliriously as Theo moved closer. *Oh god please work. Let me be wrong, let us have this. Let him touch my face. Let us have one kiss, just give us that.*

Theo lifted his hand, slow and hesitant. If Kade still had a heartbeat, it would have stopped.

Theo touched his cheek.

Kade burned.

He jolted back with a pained yell. It stung, but the disappointment was so much worse. Of *course* it didn't work. Of *course* they didn't get to have this. Kade's life was trash, had *always* been trash, why not have his afterlife carry on the grand Renfield tradition?

"Shit," Kade whispered. "Shit, shit, shit. It was for *nothing.*"

"It's fine," Theo said with a strained smile. "Kade, hey. You're fine."

"It's not FINE," Kade bellowed. "I wasn't ready yet! What was the point? What's the point of any of it if we're still stuck like this, wearing gloves and tiptoeing around each other in the kitchen so we don't accidentally touch each other? This is bullshit!"

The mug handle shattered in his hand. Kade had squeezed it to smithereens.

"Shit," Kade spat. He was breathing hard, but there was no relief. No rapid heartbeat, no sweat. Just panic swirling in his dead chest and a stinging cheek.

"Let me heal you," Theo offered.

Kade grumbled but held still. Bitterness surged through him as Theo touched him again, the pain intensifying.

Kade waited for it to ebb away, like it always did when Theo healed him. But it didn't. It grew stronger, the burn burrowing through layers of pale skin.

Theo yanked his hand away. "Why isn't it working?"

"Can't heal a dead thing, I guess!" Kade laughed harshly and stormed past him toward the door. "Come on, you said everybody's waiting! Let's go tell them it didn't work. Ritual's still on *and* we didn't stop him from getting the flower. We're one step closer to screwing over the whole town, and probably dying in the process."

He yanked open the door to find Felicity standing in the doorway, twisting a weathered strand of fire eye around her fingers. Her gaze lingered on the burn on his cheek, but only for a second.

"You're such a Debbie Downer," she told him in a terrible British accent. She smiled like she was her usual cool, mocking self. But there was a brittleness in her eyes, a relief not unlike Theo's as he watched Kade come back to himself.

Kade refused to wonder if she was worried about him. He gestured behind him at the wrecked kitchen.

"Sorry," he said.

"We'll clean it up. Don't worry about it." She tucked the fire eye away, and Kade's gaze locked onto a bandage on her wrist. This one had the smallest spot of blood against the white. Dark. Fresh. Kade's mouth watered, teeth thickening.

"Whoa." Felicity laughed, stepping back. "Put those away, man. I'm tapped out for today. Didn't even get any venom out of it."

She looked over Kade's shoulder. Kade turned to find Theo standing behind him, hands clenched at his sides, looking ready to slam him into the ground if necessary.

Kade swallowed back a tide of saliva. For a moment, it *had* felt necessary. He had completely forgotten about Felicity, and only seen the sweet blood underneath.

"Come on," Felicity said, oddly quiet. "We're through here."

Kade heard them in the hall: Milly and Skeeter talking about chess, Beverly Sloan humming distractedly as she dusted the space where a vase used to be. Sparky pacing around, desperately trying to get someone to pet him.

Then he stepped inside and everyone went silent.

Felicity cleared her throat.

"Good news is he's fine," she announced. "Bad news—"

Sparky yelped and ran over, leaping up to brace her paws on Kade's chest.

"I'm okay," he assured her, stroking her ears. He wanted to bend down and comfort her properly, but he didn't want to start sobbing in front of everyone. He was almost glad Sundance wasn't here for this.

"Ritual's still on," Felicity said. "So. There goes that plan."

"That's fine," Milly said, in that overly hopeful voice that never sounded as natural as she wanted it to be. "We can still stop Victor from gaining everything he needs. Felicity and Bev are going to check out the Emmerson place. I've been combing through local history to find anything about Cyth's dress or a spear, I'm sure I'll come up with something."

"Or we're stuck chasing our own tails," Felicity said. "Watching Victor break into houses we didn't know to be careful about, turning their teenagers for nefarious plans we still don't know the full scope of."

"Felicity," Beverly said warningly.

"*Beverly*," Felicity replied, flopping down on the couch beside Skeeter and Milly. She patted the last empty spot next to her. "Take a seat, my dead friend."

Kade tried to laugh. It came out dry and cracked. He didn't want to be here, coming up with their next plan. He wanted to go home and—well, not sleep. And he couldn't drink. He couldn't start a fight; it wouldn't hurt him and he'd have to pull all his punches.

Sparky licked his hand. He patted her absently, listening to the worried whine in her chest. It was all so *much*: the fly buzzing on the ceiling. Electricity humming in the walls and wind outside the windows. Beverly Sloan's perfume, Felicity's nervous sweat, cleaning fluids and dust where the Sloans hadn't been able to reach. Sparky's strange ozone musk and the stink of burned florals. And over it all: the thumping din of heartbeats, the overwhelming scent of blood waiting under flimsy skin. How did Theo put up with this all the time? It was maddening.

A hand on his sleeve made him jump.

"Hold your breath," Theo whispered. "It helps."

Kade nodded. He was afraid that if he opened his mouth an outraged wail would come out. Theo shouldn't be standing a careful distance away, touching Kade's shirt. He should be dragging him so close Kade couldn't tell where he ended and Theo began.

The front door opened. Kade turned toward it, distantly aware of Theo and Skeeter following suit.

Racing footsteps. A heartbeat that was familiar even though he'd never heard it before.

"Where is he?" Sundance yelled from the front hall. "Hello? Beverly?"

"He's okay, Sundance," Beverly called back. "He's in here."

The footsteps sped up. Theo's hand tightened on Kade's sleeve before inevitably dropping.

Sundance burst into the room. Sparky ran up to her, headbutting her knee, but for once Sundance didn't pat her. She just stood there, staring in growing horror at the blood drenching Theo's shirt, the burn on Kade's cheek. *Sundance is on her way,* Theo had said. What had he told her?

"I'm okay," Kade blurted. "I'm, uh. Dead. But other than that—"

Sundance blew out a watery breath and launched herself at him. Her arms folded around him, squeezing him so hard it would hurt if he was still alive.

"I'm okay," Kade repeated, resting his chin on top of her head. He'd always thought of Sundance as sturdy, but suddenly she felt so fragile in his arms. Breakable. *Human.*

Sundance sniffed, pulling back. "I thought you were saving this for the day before the ritual. I was going to make you that pudding you like."

Kade shrugged stiffly. "We thought earlier was better."

Sundance's gaze flickered once more to Theo's shirt soaked with Kade's blood. She was giving him that strained, sad look she often had when he was breaking her heart. He'd only seen it from hospital beds or bathroom floors or that time she had to coax him out from under his bed the week after his mum's funeral. It never lasted long—she was good at hiding it. He always appreciated that about her.

Sparky licked her hand. Sundance startled.

"Can't take one second where it's not about you," she muttered, stroking Sparky's head. Then she turned back to Kade, her smile more solid. "Well, you look pretty alive to me."

She hugged him again. Kade hugged back, sinking into her comforting hold.

Then, all of a sudden, the comfort was gone. In its place was a hot hunger, her heartbeat growing louder in his ears. Kade's grip tightened. His teeth sharpened, his nails following suit, digging into her work uniform—

"Okay," Theo said. "That's enough for now."

He tugged Kade away. At first Kade resisted. Then he saw Theo's alarmed face, Skeeter holding a knife she definitely didn't have before, Beverly reaching under a couch cushion like she had a crossbow hidden under there.

"Right," Kade said, dropping his arms from Sundance's suddenly frail body. He stepped back, thinking about the mug he'd shattered in Felicity's kitchen. Was this what Theo had to deal with all the time? It felt...horrifying. If Kade was going to hurt someone, he wanted it to be on purpose. Not because he forgot himself and ripped a hole in his aunt's throat.

Not to mention her work clothes, he thought, wincing as he noticed the holes he'd poked in her shirt with his nails.

Beverly cleared her throat, straightening up again. "What were you saying, Milly?"

"Well—" Milly started.

Kade cut her off. "Not that this isn't riveting. But I'm gonna go talk to Theo."

All eyes turned to him once more. Kade gritted his teeth.

"Alone," he prompted.

Theo blinked. Then he jerked into motion, following Kade into the hall.

Kade hadn't been inside the training room since he threw the Molotov cocktail. It was covered in scorch marks. Several axes had their wooden hilts burned to stubs. They hadn't had time to put everything out before they raced after Theo, tailing the distant shape of Victor in the sky.

"I'm really screwing up the Sloans' house," Kade muttered. He reached out and touched the tip of an ax blade. It burned his finger, making him jerk back. "Ow, shit!"

Theo huffed a faint laugh as he closed the door. "What are you doing?"

"Testing," Kade said, touching the burned wood. "You never tested anything after you got turned. You just let things happen."

"I tested," Theo argued. "I ate something after you

goaded me into it. Then I puked for an hour. Didn't want to test much after that."

Kade laughed. Talking Theo into trying a McDonald's fry felt like a million years ago. Then again, time always felt wrong after he came out of a vision. Slick, almost liquid. Like he could look through and see it all happening at once. Like he could dive in and never hit the bottom.

Theo asked, "What did you want to talk to me about?"

Kade swallowed. His throat was too dry, his skin stretched tight. He needed to feed. To rest. But he needed to get this over with first.

"We'll tell them," he started. "I just don't want to say it for the first time in front of everyone."

He closed his eyes. Blood, flesh, fire. He still hadn't seen their old selves die yet.

"I had a vision," he admitted. "When I...woke up. They changed the ritual. That's what the hex bag— that's what the *pouch* did. It's our fingers in there. Our bones."

Theo twitched. His fingers tightened into fists, and Kade knew he was imagining a knife slicing through his hand. He always hated talking about their past selves, hated thinking that the fates of those boys had anything to do with him.

"They changed it," Theo said, latching determinedly onto the least disturbing thing in that sentence. "What did they do?"

Kade grinned. He couldn't help it. He still felt doomed. Felt it in his marrow, the same way he'd felt it since before he could remember. And yet, the joy was there: what a *story*. A horrible, dark story of death and misfortune, but a story nonetheless.

"So," he began. "Burn me to death like Victor wants? Cyth is sealed in there forever."

Theo opened his mouth, the protest ready on his lips.

Kade cut him off. "Hey! I'm not done. Burn me to death and she's trapped. But burn me a *little* bit..." He touched his cheek, where the burn was gradually getting smaller. "The coffin opens."

"Cyth escapes," Theo said. "The ritual is over."

Kade nodded. He could see the realization forming behind Theo's eyes. That stupid, wild hope.

"And I can touch you," Theo finished.

Kade grinned shakily. "For about thirty seconds. Before they kill us and destroy the town."

Theo looked down at him. Kade didn't have to ask what he was thinking. He was thinking the same thing. For a moment all the horror and bitterness of today was gone, and Kade almost believed—*truly* believed—that everything might be okay.

Then something pulsed deep inside Kade's belly, and he shuddered. The heartbeats were distant down the hall, but he could hear them again. Calling for him to feed. His own blood on Theo's shirt was like a siren's song. He wanted to get on his knees and suck it out of the fabric.

"Kade," Theo said. "You okay?"

"I'm hungry," Kade rasped, slurring around the fangs growing in his mouth.

Theo nodded. Kade could see him trying to process everything, shutting down all the disappointment and relief and hope so he could be there for Kade.

Theo turned toward the door, stopping when Kade shuddered again. "Whoa, hey. You good?"

"Fine," Kade mumbled, fighting to stop himself from reaching out to grip Theo's sodden shirt. "It's just...a lot."

"I know." Theo smiled understandingly. "You're gonna be fine."

"Sure." Kade held his breath. It didn't help. The scent trickled through, gripping his dry throat like a vice.

He grimaced. "Theo?"

"Yes?"

"Can you change your shirt?"

"SO," Felicity said. "This is...*better*?"

Theo winced. "Yeah."

Felicity shot him a sideways look, squinting through the moonlight. "Well. That's bad news."

Theo didn't reply. He watched Skeeter and Kade as they crouched over one of the many, *many* deer that Kade had killed over the past few days. Kade kept lifting his head to snarl at Skeeter, his eyes black and vicious.

Their first hunt had ended with Theo holding Kade down until he stopped trying to wriggle free and chase a minivan into the road. Their second—because Kade had gotten hungry a mere five hours after feeding— ended with Kade punting Theo into a tree because he tried to stop him going after a hiker.

After that, Theo enlisted backup. Skeeter had been overjoyed to get out of the house every night. Even more excited to stretch her legs. She'd been less enthused about killing forest life, but by the time Kade ripped something's throat out any reluctance got overtaken by hunger.

Felicity sighed, head cocking as she watched them feed. "Look at that. Did you see them *run?* Pure freedom."

Theo frowned. *Freedom* wasn't how he would describe a hunt. Running for running's sake, maybe. He'd had some truly transcendent experiences running through the woods as fast as he dared. But not a hunt. There was no freedom in their faces when Kade brought the deer down, just hunger and something that looked oddly similar to when Kade tackled a classmate to the ground, bright and brutal. *The monster face,* Kade had said when Theo brought it up. *I didn't even have to try with that one.*

Theo asked, "Are you sure you didn't find anything suspicious at the Emmerson house? They're a hunting family, they should have *something*."

"Mom and I will go back again later. And we *won't* bring food. They didn't like it last time, it makes them feel like a funeral situation. *Our daughter's not dead, she might be totally fine,*" Felicity continued, in what Theo assumed was a mocking imitation of Mr. Emmerson.

She pulled her leg up behind her, stretching. "Sure you don't want to come? Maybe you can sniff something out."

"I will," Theo said. "I just have to...you know."

He nodded at Kade, who was growling at Skeeter again before burying his face in warm deer belly.

"Right," Felicity said, stretching her leg high. "Babysitting duty. Hey, aren't you supposed to be stocking shelves right now?"

"Called in sick."

Felicity snorted. "Again? You can't have *that* many sick days."

Theo didn't. His manager had pulled him aside during his last shift to tell him if he kept this up, he'd be out on his ass.

"Aren't you supposed to be in bed?" he asked. "You have school tomorrow."

"And miss all this?" Felicity let go of her leg and smiled. It was a surprisingly warm smile, if a little exhausted. "How's training going? Want to try to coax your wings out later?"

Theo sighed. "We can try. I'm meeting up with Milly today, seeing if she can help. I *need* to be stronger, Liss. Something that can match his monster."

Felicity hummed. "I don't know. Looks like Kade has that handled—oh, crap."

Kade was staring at her again, gore dripping off his chin. Beside him, Skeeter continued eating, unbothered.

"Yummy deer," Felicity called, reaching slowly for the knife she had strapped to her belt. "Right? Don't look at the human in the curtains. Look at that warm, ripe deer right in front of you!"

Kade bolted up, teeth bared.

Felicity yanked her knife out. "Shit."

"Shit," Theo agreed, and tackled Kade to the ground.

Kade snarled and swiped. Theo pinned him, counting down. Last time it had taken ten seconds.

"Come back," he told Kade as he growled. "Hey. None of that. It's just Liss, okay? We *like* Liss. Put the teeth away."

Slowly, Kade's growling faded.

Skeeter blurred to Theo's side, wavering awkwardly. "Is he okay? Do I help?"

"No," Theo said, politely not bringing up how she'd barely been any help since the first time, where she'd accidentally clawed Theo in the face while grabbing Kade's wrists. "I'm fine. Thanks."

Kade blinked hard. The black bled away, leaving nothing but lovely gray. He stared up at them.

Felicity waved. "Sup, snacky?"

Kade groaned, sagging against the forest floor. "Again? Liss, I told you to go *home*."

"I'm exposure therapy!" Felicity argued, sheathing her knife. "I'm *helping*. Look, Skeeter's around me all the time and she's fine! You having fun, Skeet?"

"Yeah," Skeeter said, pulling a bloody strand of hair from her mouth. "I mean. Until I remember I'm vegetarian. Then I kinda want to cry. I petted a friendly fawn last spring, I really hope that wasn't her."

"Don't pet wild animals," Theo said.

"Dude, we *murder* wild animals on a regular basis.

Let her pet one." Kade shifted in the dirt. "Gonna let me up?"

"What? Oh." Theo stood, dragging Kade up by his shirt. "Sorry."

He tried wiping Kade down. It was useless—the blood and dirt were congealing over his clothes, and Theo was wearing gloves. He knew from previous hunts: wiping his face would just smear the grime in deeper.

"How are you feeling?" Skeeter asked.

Kade shrugged. He'd been...distant, since he got turned. Theo couldn't tell if it was bloodlust or disappointment from not being able to touch Theo, or that the ritual was still on, never mind that Kade's heart had stopped beating. Whenever he asked, Kade insisted he was fine, and that Theo needed to quit bothering him about it.

Kade turned to Skeeter, who was looking sadly at a piece of deer fur she'd picked out of her teeth. "How long did it take for your hunger to calm down?"

"Oh," Skeeter said. "Um."

Her gaze darted toward Theo, who tried to look as unconcerned as possible. They'd already discussed this the day before while Kade was showering the blood off: Theo and Skeeter were never as ravenous as Kade, who was eating a dozen animals every night and still getting human blood every day. In a mug, because they didn't trust him to feed from the source yet. Theo didn't want to have to pull him off Felicity, no matter how much she complained that donating blood wasn't worth it without venom.

"I'm sure it will settle down soon," Skeeter said, sounding as convincing as Felicity pretending to be sober at a party after nine p.m.

"It's just the first week," Theo added. "It's intense."

Kade ran a hand over his short hair, grimacing when he realized he was rubbing blood through it.

"Sure," he said. "Great. Until then, I'm just...really living up to the Monster name."

A cool spring breeze washed over the forest. Only one of them shivered.

Milly set up a mirror in the least scorched part of the Sloan training room.

"Try to connect with the beast inside," she told him. "He's in there. You just have to draw him out."

Theo stared into his reflection. Same golden curls. Same strong nose and chiseled jawbone, same nonexistent stubble that would never grow out. He looked stressed. Kade was back at the house with a thermos full of raccoon blood to tide him over. It didn't feel safe sending him to school when he could hardly control himself around his aunt, let alone a hundred jeering classmates.

"It's worse for Kade," Theo said. "The bloodlust. We're hunting every night."

Milly looked up from her notebook. She'd been idly

scratching at the scar on her face, her pen shoved into the divot.

"I have a new friend in North Carolina who helps with newborns who have a harder time adjusting," she said distractedly. "He can go to her if it doesn't get better."

Theo dug his fingers into his denim-clad knees. He didn't *want* Kade to go to North Carolina. He wanted Milly to give them a fix. A cure-all. Something that would make Kade stop staring at Felicity's wrists as she tied her hair, or a passerby's sweaty neck.

Milly pushed her skull-festooned friendship bracelet higher up her arm. "What did your dad say about turning?"

"He said I needed to be what he made me," Theo said sourly. He touched his side. It was almost healed, the grooves Victor had taken out of him turning once more to smooth, dead skin.

"Vicious," he continued. "Connect with the beast. Like you said."

Milly nodded, scribbling something in her notebook. "You will need to fight. Even if we find a way to avert the ritual, he will come after you."

"I *know*," Theo said, too harsh. He swallowed, forced his tone calm. "Any news?"

Milly shook her head, her hair sticking to her collarbones. She hadn't been washing it lately.

"I've been trying to figure out how your mother's

involved. I've read about vampires being starved for long periods of time, it takes them a while to bounce back. And you can't raze a town if you're that weak. *And* she's been burning with magic fire for centuries, *that* can't help. She'll need some way to get back to her full strength."

"A new body," Theo supplied, heart sinking. "You think she's a vessel."

"Maybe." Milly scratched her scar again, pausing her pen as she noticed the look on his face. "Or I could be wrong. I didn't guess anything about reincarnation, it's entirely possible the theory is—"

"Okay," Theo snapped. "*Thanks*, or whatever. Just help me focus."

Milly set her notebook down and stared at the page, her white eye twitching. Her voice was deeper and oddly faraway. Like she was speaking to him from the end of a long tunnel.

"Tune into your rage," she said. "Into your hunger."

Theo stared into his reflection. Those damn blond curls. The haughty expression he fell into when he was pissed off. He was a Fairgood, for better or worse. Might as well use that to his advantage. Might as well make him something other than a tool to be used.

"Tune into the thing scratching inside of you," Milly continued.

Theo tried to feel the scratch. Nothing happened. He closed his eyes, conjuring wings itching inside his shoulders, his bones lengthening and snapping into strange new shapes. Claws pressing inside his fingers, wanting out.

He *needed* to do this. To be as big as his father. To be just as tall and spindly and wicked. Something to match his horrible bulk. He'd tried to give into it for so long: hiding his soft parts, pulling up a sneer instead of an apology, making his parents proud. Now he had to put the soft parts away again, drag the viciousness out a while longer.

Just for a night. Long enough to kill his dad. Then he could be New Theo again, who held his boyfriend's hand in the halls and carried a mushroom identifying booklet in his backpack and didn't join in on the laughter when someone tripped in the halls.

"Become what you must be," Milly said, her voice thick and wrong.

For a moment, Theo felt it: an itch, right over his heart.

He opened his eyes.

His reflection stared back at him. Same harmless curls, same brown eyes. Milly sat across from him, blinking rapidly. Her pen had snapped in two.

"Ah," she said, frowning down at the ink stain on her hand. She wiped it on her shirt and cleared her throat. "How are things with Sparky?"

Theo glowered at his useless reflection. "About as good as this."

. . .

Two hours later he was in the woods again, throwing a stick.

Sparky ran for it, tongue lolling happily out of her mouth. She leapt, stretching out to grab it out of the air.

"Stop," Theo called.

Sparky hesitated. The stick clattered onto the forest floor, Sparky following it forlornly.

Theo sighed. "You're meant to ignore me! Do what *you* want."

Sparky gave him an uncertain look and picked up the stick. He didn't need a psychic link to interpret that look: *you want me to obey you SOMETIMES. But not OTHER times. This is all so confusing.*

"I know it's weird," Theo said, bending down as she came plodding back. "We just need to be prepared for the next time he tries to command you. If you can't disobey *me*, what chance do you have with the guy who has a mind-control switch in your brain?"

Sparky whined and dropped the stick into his lap.

Theo took it. "I know he made you. But that doesn't mean you let him take you over. Follow your heart. Where's it pointing?"

Sparky barked happily and took off.

Theo turned to find Kade emerging through the trees, hauling Sparky easily into his arms for a kiss. He hadn't made any noise. Theo would miss his heavy step, a noise as constant as Kade's heartbeat. But it was still undeniably Kade, even if Theo couldn't hear him coming anymore.

Kade lowered Sparky and picked up the stick near Theo's feet, tossing it out of sight. "Go fetch."

Sparky took off, barking.

Theo kissed Kade's gloved palm. "How are you feeling?"

"Great," Kade replied flatly, lowering their joined hands to drum the thermos of blood clipped to his belt. "How'd monster training go?"

Theo laughed. "Do you see any wings?"

Kade made a show of checking Theo's back. He was more graceful now that he was dead. His movements were smoother, faster. His scars were gone—Any evidence of a lifetime sticking himself with sewing needles and getting into fights wiped clean when his heart stopped. So was Theo's kiss scar, and the burn Kade refused to let Theo heal after the Hawthorn fight. The only thing that remained was his eyebrow, the split never growing back after Theo accidentally burned it. Theo often caught Kade stroking it in the mirror. When Theo asked him about it, he admitted that he was hoping he'd get to keep the kiss scar.

"I felt something," Theo said. "I just need to tune into it. Get properly vicious, one last time."

"Maybe I should try. I'm more connected to my viciousness nowadays." Kade pulled his lips back, showing off his fangs. He said it sarcastically, but there was something bitter underneath it. The same panic that came whenever he blinked back to himself to find Theo holding him back from ravaging some innocent hiker.

"You're just hungry," Theo told him.

Kade huffed, looking into the trees.

Theo squeezed his hand. "What?"

"Nothing." Kade chewed his lip, the strip of skin growing back the second he scraped it off. "I just—I don't know. Wish we could be who we wanna be already."

It was so quiet and honest that Theo was taken aback.

"What do we want to be?"

Kade smirked. "Soft. Peaceful. I know I'm all—" He waved at his outfit, his wallet chain and ripped clothes and single dagger earring. "But you know me. I want to be soft. And yours. I want to be other things, obviously, but those are the main two."

He scuffed a boot in the dirt, the movement blurring inhumanly fast. But still Kade. Still the sweet, lovely boy Theo had tried not to fall for and failed miserably. He was gone for Kade before he brought him a pair of replacement knitting needles.

Kade rolled his eyes. "What? Quit looking at me like that."

"Not looking at you like anything," Theo said quietly.

He dropped Kade's hand. Any longer and the urge to lean in would become physically painful. He missed

Kade's soft metallic scent, which was so much stronger when he was alive. He missed watching Kade sleep—it was the only time he was totally relaxed. He missed cooking for Kade and biting into his beautiful neck. He missed Kade's blood, the best thing he'd ever tasted. But he still had Kade—that was what mattered.

"We need to do something normal," Theo announced. "Something that isn't monster training and Sparky training and hunting and trying to figure out where the last ritual ingredients are."

This finally coaxed a proper laugh out of Kade. "How the tables turn! Remember when it was me desperately trying to make you chill out for five seconds?"

Theo laughed awkwardly. He still couldn't talk much about the weeks following his dad's 'death.' He didn't like who he had turned into.

"Movie night?" he suggested. "Popcorn, action movies, Felicity can paint your nails—"

"Sure! Yeah. We can hunt early, then...yeah." Kade bit his lip hard, the skin sealing back into place under his teeth as he looked into the trees. Sparky was coming back, her paws beating loud on the forest floor.

"Totally normal movie night," Kade finished. "Awesome."

CHAPTER
SIXTEEN

IT WAS the first time Kade had been alone in a room with Skeeter, and the silence was becoming unbearable.

He glanced hopefully toward the living room. Theo had said he was going to pick a DVD from the Sloans' old-school collection, which surely wouldn't take long. But they'd been here for several minutes already, and Theo hadn't followed him into the kitchen.

"Soooo," Kade said as the tin foil finally started to expand over the popcorn pan. "Like, you can hang out with Liss and it doesn't affect you at all?"

Skeeter blinked at him. She had a finger in her mouth, gnawing the nail. Kade wondered if she, too, had discovered that nail-chewing got even more disgusting when they grew back so fast. No more careless nibbles. It was a dedicated chew, every time.

"Pretty much," she said. "So, um. What are you doing for college?"

"Huh?"

"I just don't know much about you," Skeeter continued apologetically. "I just thought...um, never mind."

"No, it's fine." Kade blinked hard, jumping tracks from the vampire crap that had been consuming his life for a year and back to normal life shit. That was what they were doing this for, right? Normal. Mundane. Taking their mind off the imminent doom.

"I want to try fashion school," Kade admitted. "Maybe."

He braced himself for a snicker. But Skeeter brightened.

"Oh, cool! Felicity said you do all your own clothes. Some of Theo's, too. I'm going to apply for some out of state schools and see if I can get scholarships. I don't know what I'll major in yet. Mom says I should go to law school, but that sounds like a lot. If I don't get scholarships I'll just stay in town and work a while. Save some money."

She bit her lip, falling quiet. Kade had never heard her talk so much at once. When they were in the woods together, they had to stay quiet so they didn't chase the animals away.

"It's weird," she said shyly, as if she expected Kade to shut her down any moment now. "This time last month I was worried about if I should take up a sport to make my extracurriculars look good to colleges."

"Your extracurriculars are already pretty damn

good," Kade said, thinking about the debate club and the chess club and a few other clubs Felicity had mentioned while Kade wasn't paying attention, instead watching Felicity's blood drain from her wrist into a mug.

"You could do a sport," Kade continued. "You could be a pro athlete."

Skeeter sighed. "It wouldn't be real. And I don't know if sports are for me anyway. Last time I played a team sport I told our goalie I was going to sue her for being so bad at her job."

Kade laughed at her embarrassed expression. "Shit. Maybe you *should* be a lawyer."

She stared at him. Then she ducked her head, turning to the popcorn pan again. Kade shrank back, assuming it was a signal that the conversation was over. Did she think his laugh was weird? Both Theo and Felicity had admitted they were surprised when Kade had a laugh that was different from the harsh, contemptuous bark he'd let out at school. Until recently, nobody except Sundance had heard his stupid giggle in a very long time.

The tin foil swelled, popcorn crackling underneath. Kade's fingers twitched as he thought of burns and flowers and death.

Skeeter asked, "Why aren't you this nice at school?"

Kade stared at her, lost for words.

Skeeter winced apologetically. "At school you're always, um, growly? You kind of freaked me out, honestly. Theo too, for different reasons. Now you're...I don't know. You're pretty cool."

She shrugged again, shoulders climbing like she wanted to vanish into them. Kade could relate—something about that small compliment made him want to find a dark corner to hide in. He didn't get a lot of compliments. He still got flustered when Theo said something nice about him, to Theo's continued delight.

Kade cleared his throat. "Yeah, well. Gotta play up the Monster persona, right? Otherwise the fair folk of Lock High will walk all over me."

"Um. Sure." She gave him a timid smile. "It just... sounds kind of tiring."

Kade almost laughed again. His school laugh, dark and bitter. He'd been shoved around his whole life, so he'd turned himself into something sharp so at least he could have the satisfaction of watching them bleed. It was exhausting, being something people cut themselves on.

"No offense," Skeeter continued, biting her continuously regrowing nails again, the polish long since gnawed off.

Kade opened his mouth to insist it was fine. Then he froze.

Blood in the air. Just a little bit, but enough to make his mouth water.

"What?" Skeeter asked.

Kade forced a smile. "You don't smell that?"

"Smell what?" Skeeter paused, cocking her head.

"Oh. Felicity must've hurt herself again. She trains *really* hard, I keep telling her to cool it."

The pan let out a worrying pop.

"Oh damn." Skeeter lurched toward the popcorn.

Kade watched her lift it off the stovetop, despairing. Why was he still so *hungry*? Why did a faint whiff of blood make him spiral when Skeeter barely noticed it, humming as she bustled around the kitchen grabbing a bowl for the popcorn only one of them was able to eat?

The tantalizing scent drifted closer. Voices came with it, Theo's tense and trying not to be, Felicity's dismissive and impatient.

Kade gripped the countertop behind him.

"I told you, I like my scars," Felicity said as she reached the kitchen doorway, holding a chocolate protein shake. Her hair was wet and she had on the baggy sushi PJs she wore when she was bloated. Yet another bandage gleamed on her upper arm, specks of red dotting the white fabric.

Kade held his breath. It didn't help. The scent invaded him anyway, crawling down his throat and squeezing his dead heart. He didn't just want it, he *needed* it. No matter how much he told himself he was full, he knew what he needed, and it was right under Felicity's scarred skin, waiting for him to—

"Babe," Theo said. "Watch the strength."

Kade blinked. Theo was standing in front of him, smiling stiffly. He was holding a *Rocky Horror* DVD, thanks to Beverly Sloan having Opinions on preserving physical media.

Theo motioned behind him. Kade turned.

The countertop behind him was cracked. Ten dents from Kade's sharp, hard fingers.

"Shit," Kade said. "Sorry."

"We're gonna remodel in the fall anyway," Felicity said with a hesitant grin. "You're basically helping us."

She tugged at her bandage, her grin brightening when she noticed the bowl Skeeter was holding. "Aw, popcorn for the token human? I'm touched!"

"You have to eat all of it," Skeeter said, in a weird voice that made Kade feel he was missing an inside joke.

"So you can live vicariously through me? Ugh, I *guess*." Felicity tucked her protein shake under her arm and swiped the bowl, throwing a handful of popcorn into her mouth. "Come on, gang. Night's a'wasting, and I have a lot of nails to get through."

She reached for Kade's hand, possibly to critique how his were always peeling.

Kade stepped back so fast he backed into the counter. The sink rattled behind him, metal buckling.

Kade winced. The Sloans were rich, they could replace whatever he'd just broken. He just wished he could stop breaking their house.

"I'm actually gonna go for a walk," he said, too loud. "I need some air."

"No you don't," Felicity said, looking utterly unconcerned by the state of her kitchen.

"Figure of speech, Liss."

"Well, we can't put it off," Felicity said. "Me and Mom are going to the Emmerson house at eight."

"That's tonight?"

"Yup. Mom's distracting, I'm sneaking. Hopefully I find something more useful than the dad's eighties porn collection this time."

Kade rubbed his forehead, trying to shove down the persistent pulse emanating under Felicity's warm skin. "Whatever. Start the movie without me, I've seen it already."

He tried to ignore Theo's worried gaze as he stepped past him, but Theo caught his sleeve.

"I'm fine, sunshine," Kade lied. "Promise. I just need a smoke."

Theo frowned. "Do you want me to come with you?"

"Nope," Kade said, and sauntered out.

He paced through the woods, chain-smoking cigarettes. One for every long inhale.

"Shit," he whispered, crushing a seventh cigarette under his boot. "Shit, shit, bloody goddamn *shit*."

He shelled out another cigarette, hand shaking as he lit up. He wanted to go back into Felicity's kitchen and start smashing things. He wanted to grab Theo and shake him, yell at him that he didn't need to be watched like a puppy who might piss on the carpet. Or, y'know, savage the next person to walk past. He wanted to sink his fangs into something, he wanted to rip it apart. Most of it wasn't even bloodlust. It was just *Kade*, that old Renfield urge to destroy everything around him and then himself. It was older than the hunger. It had been here before he even existed—

A low, shitty whistle pulled Kade out of his thought spiral.

Finn Harley was strolling through the woods, a shovel slung over his shoulder and a determined look on his stupid, smug face.

Kade ducked behind a thick tree before Finn could notice him.

"What the hell?" He muttered. The last time *he* went into the woods with a shovel, it was to bury Mr. Fletcher. Everybody was staying out of the woods since high schoolers started getting kidnapped, and Finn was prancing through, devil-may-care? Something was up.

Kade pulled out his phone and started typing: *FINN DOING WEIRD SHIT IN THE WOODS, COME NOW.*

He hit send. A reply came in less than ten seconds later:

Coming. Don't do anything stupid til I get there.

"Right," Kade whispered. "I'll just save the stupid until after you show up. Thanks, babe."

Finn stopped. Tilted his head.

Kade froze. He didn't say it *that* loud, right? He was too far away for Finn to hear that. There was no way—

Finn hoisted the shovel, waving ineffectually.

"Hey!" he called. "I thought I was gonna have to find it on my own. Am I close? I brought the shovel!"

A warm, friendly voice echoed through the woods, filling Kade with dread.

"I can see that," said Carol Fairgood as she stepped into view. She was wearing a peach pantsuit, her hair styled into her husband's trademark curls, which Kade had never seen her without.

"You're close," she continued. "A little bit this way."

"Cool," said Finn easily.

Kade tailed them, reeling. Finn was acting so *normal*; did he know what was going on? Was he a psychopath who was totally okay with whatever freaky shit Carol was leading him toward? She *had* to be leading him somewhere bad, why else would Victor's second-in-command be out in the woods with Finn Harley on a random school day evening?

"Sooo," Finn said after an awkwardly silent walk, struggling under the weight of the shovel. "How was your trip?"

"Invigorating," she replied, coming to a stop on a seemingly innocuous patch of forest floor. "You can start here."

"Cool!" Finn stopped, letting the shovel fall off his shoulder. He took a second to stretch, muscles popping before he picked the shovel back up, holding it like he'd never dug a hole in his damn life. He drove the blade into the dirt, glaring accusingly when it only earned him a tiny spoonful of dirt.

"Thanks for this," Finn continued, grunting with effort. "I was going to have to jump through *so* many hoops, you have no idea. People will be talking about this party *forever*."

"Fingers crossed," Carol replied.

Kade got out his phone again. His fingers were shaking. Was it the spear under that dirt? The dress? Some other shit they had no clue they should've been looking for? How did he even *phrase* this? *Hey babe, your mom's back in town. No, she didn't come to see you, she's helping some kid dig a hole in the woods for dubiously nefarious purposes. I'm crouching in some bushes twenty feet away, hurry up.*

But before he could press send, an overwhelming scent made him freeze.

He looked up, dead stomach filling with dread as he saw exactly what he'd been expecting.

Finn examined his finger, annoyed. The smallest drop of blood beaded on his fingertip.

"Shit," he sighed.

Carol looked up. She had been examining the forest, scanning in a way that made Kade instantly nervous.

"What is it?"

"Nothing. Just cut myself. Shoveling is *hard*." Finn shook his hand. A drop of blood landed in the dirt.

"Not that hard," he continued. "Like, I can *do* it..."

The rest of Finn's defense faded out, replaced by his deafeningly loud heartbeat slamming in Kade's ears.

Don't, Kade begged.

But he could feel the monster inside him baring its teeth. Could feel his own body betraying him, his new instincts taking over as he dropped into a crouch. Could hear himself growling, snarling, ready to destroy something.

Ready to hunt.

CHAPTER
SEVENTEEN

"SO," Theo said. "What are the rumors?"

Felicity snorted, bending low over Skeeter's hand to brush purple glitter over her thumbnail. "You ran away together. *Or* you and Aaron and Kade did a murder-murder-suicide."

"Who did what?" Skeeter asked.

"They can't decide. Last vote is that Aaron killed Theo, so Kade killed Aaron and then himself," Felicity said distractedly. She frowned, tidying up a shred of polish that had escaped the confines of Skeeter's thumbnail.

Theo cocked his head, trying to hear Kade walking around outside. Then he stopped, feeling like an idiot. Kade walked silently now. He had no heartbeat to focus on. He could be anywhere, and Theo wouldn't know until he shouted.

He turned back to the screen, where lightning

flashed over a dark castle. "No one's seen the Fletchers?"

"Nope," Felicity said, staring at Skeeter's nails with an intensity that meant she was pouring any conflicted feelings she might have about that into making Skeeter's nails look nice.

"Maybe they left town," Skeeter suggested hopefully.

Felicity laughed. "The town they've vowed to save? The town that's relying on them and their destiny-laden bloodline, the last ones standing between Lock and complete destruction at the hands of the evil, evil vampires? I doubt it!" She frowned, bending lower over Skeeter's hand. "Shit. Smudged it. Stay still."

"I'm still," said Skeeter, affronted. It was true: she wasn't even breathing.

Theo's phone vibrated. He took it out and idly glanced down from the TV screen. It was from Kade.

FINN DOING WEIRD SHIT IN THE WOODS, COME NOW.

Theo bolted up.

Felicity cursed. "Shit! You almost made me spill!"

Theo ignored her, running for his shoes. "I need to go. Kade's following Finn, he's doing something weird in the woods."

Felicity put the nail polish aside and stood. "Got it. Let's go."

"You won't be able to keep up."

"You can piggyback me," Felicity suggested.

Skeeter stood, holding her polished fingers uncertainly at her sides. "Um. Am I coming?"

"We can handle it." Felicity leaned over her and stuffed a hand down the couch. She pulled out a small ax, tossing Theo a defiant look. "What? Come on, let's go find out what this asshole's up to."

Theo paused to send a reply. Then he scooped her up and blurred toward the back door.

He heard it as soon as they left the house: digging. Heavy and scraping, Finn muttering grudgingly as he heaved.

Felicity squeezed him from behind, her chin digging into his shoulder. "What is it?"

He shushed her and took off. Felicity grunted, but otherwise stayed shockingly silent as Theo sped into the forest. He almost stumbled when he heard another noise under the digging.

"Fingers crossed," said Carol Fairgood, her voice cool and friendly as ever.

Theo stumbled to a stop. He could see her through the trees, tapping through her phone and then looking up to scan the tree line and reply to Finn's stupid comments.

Felicity whispered, "Is that your *mom?*"

Theo didn't reply. He hated how relieved he was. Part of her had been convinced she was dead, or Victor had done something awful to her.

Felicity leaned in. "Why the hell—?"

Theo shushed her. There was a third noise: growling. Sharp and unmistakable. Theo had heard that same growl many times over the last few days.

Theo turned. About thirty yards away stood the love of his death. Eyes black, fangs out. Sprinting toward Finn with the narrow-minded abandon of a beast about to feed.

"Shit," Theo whispered, and broke into a run so suddenly that Felicity gasped and gripped his shoulders.

Kade was so distracted by the blood he didn't even notice Theo until Theo was on top of him. Theo tried to do it quietly, grabbing instead of tackling, but there was only so quiet you could be about restraining a hungry vampire.

He wrestled Kade into the dirt. Felicity climbed off him, shoving her jacket into Kade's mouth to stifle his feral growls. But the damage was done: Finn's voice echoed through the trees, thin and reedy.

"Hello?"

Kade growled through Felicity's jacket.

"Shut up," Theo whispered, shoving him harder into the dirt. Kade kept trying to snap at him, even with his mouth stuffed with fabric.

"It's cool," he heard Finn tell Carol. "I'll protect us."

"I appreciate that," Carol said.

Finn raised his voice. "I totally have a gun! So screw off!"

Theo made a face. How did Finn sound so unthreatening when he was lying about having a gun? This was why Aaron and Theo never let him hang out with them.

"Sorry," Finn added.

"No apologies needed," Carol said soothingly. "I know how teenage boys can be."

Theo frowned, still holding Kade down. He *never* swore in front of his parents. They always said that cursing indicated an uneducated mind.

"Make sure he doesn't spit it out," Theo whispered to Felicity. Then he leaned up and peered through the trees.

Finn was still digging, sweating with the effort. He looked at Carol, trying to hide how hard he was panting.

"Think I found it," he announced. He dropped the shovel and crouched down in the dirt.

Theo squinted. Finn was hauling up...a sack? It was burlap and brown. Then a chunk of dirt fell off and Theo realized it wasn't brown, the sack had just been underground so long the dirt had melded to the fabric. It was old enough to belong to a vampire who had been underground for centuries.

"Is it the dress?" Felicity whispered. "Or the spear?"

"I can't tell," Theo whispered back. "It definitely doesn't look spear shaped. Maybe it's the dress but there's other stuff shoved in there with it?"

"Shit," Felicity said. "How's your mom?"

Theo didn't reply, his dead heart clenching in his chest. Even knowing what she'd agreed to, even after watching her do nothing while her husband slammed Theo into the floor so hard the floorboards cracked, Theo still wanted to run out of his hiding place and hug her. To shake her until she saw sense. *He's lying to you, don't you get that? He's using you just like he's using me. Don't let him. I love you, mom.*

Carol stood back, letting Finn haul the bag onto the forest floor. "You're sure they don't suspect?"

"Nope," Finn said confidently.

"And you're not engaging with them. Right?"

Finn hesitated. He straightened, dusting off his hands with a nervous laugh. "You said to be normal. So...I've been normal. Talked to Kade a couple times. And I invited them to my birthday party, like you said!"

"Mm. Calmly?"

"I'm calm," Finn argued. "I'm just, y'know. Excited."

"Well, be excited *quietly*. We can't have you tip them off because you let something slip. Alright? Remember what you get out of this."

"I do," Finn said hastily. His anxious smile slipped, and for the first time Theo saw a glimpse of something serious under his eagerness. "Really. I can't tell you how grateful I am for this—this *incredible* opportunity, Mrs. Fairgood. I won't waste it."

"You'd better not," Carol said smoothly. She checked her watch and turned to leave. "Come on. It's getting dark."

"Right," Finn said. He picked up the bag again, trying to lift with his back before almost falling over and awkwardly lifting with his knees instead. Then he picked up the shovel, hunched over with the strain.

"Anything else you need," Finn rasped as he wobbled after her. "I can help. You have that thing coming up, right? At the Emmerson house?"

Carol stared at him. Then she laughed, stiff and tittering. It was the laugh she used when she was trying to hide how annoyed she was. "Oh, you heard that, did you? We'll be fine. Thank you."

They both froze as a high yelp rang through the woods.

Theo looked down.

Felicity was bleeding, clutching her wrist. Her phone lay in the dirt beside her, a text half finished. Kade had managed to spit the jacket out and had swiped a chunk of Felicity's wrist.

"Cut it out!" Theo knelt harder on Kade's chest, stuffing the jacket back into place.

Finn's voice floated through the trees. "What was that?"

"No idea," Carol said slowly. "But it sounded...hurt."

Theo waited, gritting his teeth. He hated how *thoughtful* she sounded. Like she was wondering if her husband had followed her out there, eating unsuspecting high schoolers. *Had* he followed her out there? Was he hiding in the trees, waiting to pounce?

Theo listened, projecting further than Kade's growls and his mother's heartbeat. Bugs, wind, leaves. Nothing big and horrible in the undergrowth. No rasp of dry skin or flap of wings. Just footsteps, noisy and hesitant and human as Finn followed Carol out of the woods.

Theo and Felicity hunched over in tense silence, waiting it out. Kade struggled under them, growls muffled by the ruined jacket. Felicity's bleeding arm trembled as she picked her phone up.

Theo gripped her wrist, concentrating. The smell of blood got a little more manageable.

He waited for the footsteps to fade. "You good?"

"Yeah. This *sucks* without venom." Felicity pulled her hand out of his grip and examined the healed skin. "I texted my mom, she's on her way. We need to get to the Emmerson place."

"One thing at a time." Theo wiped his bloody hand clean on Felicity's shirt and tapped Kade's shirt. "Kade. Hey! Look at me. Time to come back."

Kade writhed, bucking up against Theo's hold.

Theo sighed. "Liss, do you want to step away a second? Might be better without..."

He gestured at her stained clothes, blood already congealing under her nails.

Felicity frowned at Kade and started tiptoeing through the trees.

Theo turned back to Kade, bending close. "Kade. Babe. Come back already. You're missing out on *Rocky Horror*."

Slowly, Kade's growls quietened. He blinked hard, the black draining out of his eyes. His mouth went slack.

Theo pulled the jacket away. "Kade?"

"Bloody hell," Kade croaked. He smacked his lips, staring at Theo and the spit-covered jacket in confusion. "What happened to Finn? And your mom? Did I—?"

Theo cut him off. "They didn't see you."

"How's your mom? What was in the hole?"

"She's fine. He got a bag out of the hole, we don't know what was in it."

Kade groaned and sagged back against the dirt. Then he stopped, tongue moving in his cheeks.

"Did I *bite* Liss?"

"I'm fine," Felicity said, emerging through the trees with her fingers flying over her phone screen. "Snacky little jackass. I fed you *yesterday*."

She said it lightly, but Kade's face twisted up in that same anguished expression he got when he started thinking about the prophecy. Or his parents. Or anything that added to his bone-deep belief that he was doomed, had been doomed all along, even before he was born. That his story was an unhappy one and Theo was a sweet, naive fool for thinking it could be anything else.

"It's fine," Theo told him. "Everybody's okay."

"Not for long," Felicity said, looking up from her phone. "Mom! Over here!"

Theo and Kade turned to watch Beverly Sloan jog up, a duffel bag thrown over her shoulder and a wicked knife in her belt. She had a shockingly light step—

from her childhood as a ballerina, Felicity told him once.

Beverly came to a graceful stop, tensing her jaw when she noticed the blood streaking all three teens. "What happened?"

"Nothing," said Felicity and Theo.

"Me," said Kade bitterly. He was slurring, fangs still not completely gone. His claws flexed in his jeans, boring new holes in the denim.

"Everybody's okay," Theo repeated. "Whose car are we taking?"

Beverly sighed. She looked at Felicity pointedly, the two of them having a silent stare-off with a lot of eyebrow work until Felicity finally gave in.

"You're not coming," she told them. "If Kade still can't keep his monster down—"

"Hey, he's doing *great*," Theo snapped.

Beverly gave him an unreadable look. The one she gave Kade was much easier to interpret: wariness. A little bit of pity, enough to make Kade hunch into his shoulders. *I'd rather be punched than pitied*, he had told Theo last year. Theo had agreed wholeheartedly.

"This isn't an argument," Felicity said. She stalked up to join her mother, in sync in a way Theo had only seen when they were training together. "There's a reason we don't bring Sparky along to this stuff, right? I'd die for that dog, but bringing her to a battle is like giving the enemy an extra fighter!"

"That's not the same," Theo tried.

Felicity laughed, holding up her ripped, bloody sleeve. "Like hell it isn't! If Victor shows up, we don't have time to fight Kade off if I get a papercut! Kade, go home. Theo, make sure he doesn't eat his aunt."

"I don't need babysitting," Kade said quietly. But it sounded uncertain, like he was only saying it because he thought he should, not because he believed it. He had that doomed look again, deep and troubled and breaking Theo's goddamn heart.

He opened his mouth to argue his boyfriend's defense. To say they were wasting time, they needed to leave. But Beverly cut him off.

"Theo," she said. "Take him home. Get some rest. You've had...a tiring night."

The pity was aimed at him now. Theo's fists clenched. No need to ask whether Felicity had mentioned his mom in her texts.

"Call us if there's any trouble," he said.

They nodded. Theo watched them head back through the trees, Beverly reaching into her duffel bag to hand her daughter a silver crossbow.

He looked at Kade, who was standing so close Theo could reach out and touch his hand. Kade's teeth were finally blunt again, and his expression was so far away that for a moment Theo worried he'd fallen into a dead boy's memory again.

"Kade," he said. "You okay?"

"What?" Kade blinked hard, the smallest shudder working through him. "Yeah. Let's...let's go *rest*."

KADE HAD NEVER BEEN LESS restful in his life.

He knew Theo felt the same. He *had* to. But he was pulling this stupid display of *resting*: unknotting Kade's yarn for him, his vacant gaze on a David Attenborough documentary. All for Kade's benefit, of course. Kade could see him twitching to do something *useful*, but he would keep unknotting yarn if he thought it made Kade feel better. They didn't take care of themselves, but they always took care of each other.

Sparky headbutted Kade's knee, whining curiously.

"I'm fine," Kade assured her, tapping the fourth thermos of blood Theo had gotten for him since they got home. "I'm *resting*."

"You're pacing," Theo said without looking up. "Sit down. I got your favorite knitting needles."

Kade growled. It felt satisfying in a way it never did

when he was alive, his vocal cords finally capable of the viciousness he had been aiming for all these years. He did it again, Sparky's whining getting louder underneath it.

"We don't know if it'll happen tonight," Theo reminded him. "They might just do another reconnaissance mission. See if they can find something."

"Yeah, the *last* thing." Kade stopped, digging his fingers through the holes he'd clawed in his jeans back in the woods. "I can't believe you let them run off with that bag! When your enemies drag a mysterious bag out of the woods and you know they need two more things to complete their dark ritual, newsflash, you grab it off of them!"

"We were distracted," Theo replied, voice tight.

Kade snapped his jaw shut. He could feel his fangs form around his tongue, which was ridiculous. There was no blood around, unless you counted Sparky, who had weird, sludgy blood that smelled bad. This wasn't about hunger—that constant dull thud that never went away no matter how much Kade fed—this was just his monster coming out. He still couldn't trigger his venom and he sucked at flying and he flew off the handle at the first drop of blood, and yet some parts of vampirism felt natural in a way very few things did. But natural the same way poison was natural. Recoiling from a punch. Blood flowing from a wound.

"Hey," Theo said.

Kade blinked. Theo was standing closer all of a sudden, the yarn forgotten on the couch.

"Let's try flying again," Theo continued.

Kade sighed. They'd tried that once, their first sleepless night together.

"I never got more than an inch off the ground," Kade said sourly, forcing his teeth blunt again. "Not exactly Peter-Panning it."

"We can try again." Theo took his hands, both safely gloved, and led him into the bedroom.

"Come on," he said, closing the door so Sparky couldn't follow. "Just focus."

Kade didn't want to focus. Kade wanted to bite something. He wanted to cry. He wanted to get wasted and get into a fight, a *real* one, bruises swelling and his mouth all cut up on the inside, stinging for days after. He wanted to kiss his goddamn boyfriend. But if he couldn't take that, he'd take flying.

"Fine," he muttered. "Remind me how to do it again? Oh, right. *You just do it.*"

"Look, I don't *know*. You just..." Theo looked at the ceiling where he'd pinned Kade the first day of being dead. *Effortless*, he'd said. *I didn't even think about it.*

"Your body gets lighter," he said. "You feel...power-ful. It tingles a little. Try closing your eyes."

Kade glared. But his eyes drifted shut, his arms crossed firmly over his chest.

Theo tapped his elbows. "Might want to loosen up."

"This is as loose as I get right now," Kade snapped.

Silence. Kade squeezed his eyes shut, willing his eyes to get less watery. All that time watching Theo ignore him at school, wishing Theo would be sweet to him, and Kade was screwing it up. Why did he have to ruin everything? He had this one glimpse of happiness before everything came crashing down on him, and instead of enjoying it, he was dragging Theo through the mud with him. Destroying something good, like he always did.

Theo touched his shoulder with a gloved hand. The gentleness of it startled Kade, his eyes flying open.

"We're having fun," Theo said, like it was a decision they'd already agreed on. "Cool vampire powers. Right?"

"Right," Kade said after a moment. He let out a breath, his shoulders forcibly deflating. "Light thoughts. Okay."

Theo drifted into the air, tugging gently on Kade's jaw.

"Come on," he said. "Join me."

Kade bit his lip, trying to squash the pitiful hope. He had grown up wishing for magic. For adventure and drama and fate. Now it had happened, and the story was proving darker than he'd hoped. He needed some light.

"Doing great," Theo said.

"Shut up," Kade told him. But it was tinged with longing. He needed this. He *deserved* this. For all that Theo complained about being a vampire, there *were* some good bits, and goddammit, Kade should get to have them too.

Theo opened his mouth, probably about to give another weak encouragement. Then he stopped.

Kade felt his feet lift off the carpet. His legs tingled with lightness, at the freedom from gravity. Slowly, haltingly, he rose in the air until he was face-to-face with Theo.

"Oh shit," Kade whispered, suddenly aware of a gentle pressure on his head as his short hair skimmed the ceiling. "Oh *man*. Oh *wow*. I'm flying!"

"You're flying," Theo agreed.

They grinned at each other. This was what they'd both been hoping for when they talked about turning Kade: giddy excitement, the light in Kade's eyes just as bright as when he was alive.

The tension drained out of Kade's body with each passing second. He felt like he was full of bubbles, and also like he might cry. From gratitude this time, more than anything else. He didn't get a lot, but he got to have this.

"Race you." Kade took off across the room, pinwheeling his arms.

Theo laughed and followed. It was easy to catch up to Kade, who was moving through the air like this was a breaststroke competition.

"Hey, you," Theo said, floating over him.

Kade grinned, turning in midair to face him. "You got me!"

"See? It's like you always said." Theo leaned in, flicking his hair into Kade's face. "Being a vampire isn't all doom and gloom. We get superspeed. Super strength. We get to fly. We get black blood, which is—"

"Totally goth," Kade finished. "Thank you. I—I really needed this."

He thought about flying away. Keeping the chase going. But Theo was staring at him so softly, and Kade wanted a hundred impossible things and he couldn't have any of them.

Except this.

He concentrated and floated up until Theo had no choice but to press himself into the ceiling. Their chests brushed.

"Careful," Theo reminded him quietly.

"I know." Kade curled his fingers into Theo's belt loops. "I just...I want to pretend it worked. For a second."

Theo nodded distractedly. His pupils were so big Kade could see himself in them.

Kade wet his lips. Surely now was the time to bring up the mortifying, no-touching sex ventures he'd been thinking about.

"Theo," he whispered.

"Kade," Theo replied.

Kade's throat worked. He paused, letting himself imagine it. But his mind quickly turned to impossible things: the soft, giving plush of Theo's lips. Running his bare hands through those curls, his broad shoulders.

Touching him, *truly* touching him, no burns or goddamn gloves in the way.

"Kade," Theo repeated. "What is it?"

Kade shook his head, his dead heart squeezed in his chest. All his giddy joy from before vanished, replaced with that same bitterness from before. He didn't want to have sex with Theo if they both had to hold back. And what good was flying when he couldn't have what he really wanted? When he'd probably ruin it if he had it? He wanted Theo to be sweet to him, and he was being an ass in return. He wanted to be a vampire, and it *sucked*—no pun intended. He wanted to be in a story, but he never specified the genre, and now it might kill him before he ever got to kiss his goddamn boyfriend.

"Shit," he whispered.

Theo frowned. "What's wrong?"

"I want a cigarette," Kade blurted.

"Oh." Theo blinked, his pupils returning to a manageable size. "Okay."

Kade tried to fly back down. He lost it halfway through and landed on the ground with a hard thump.

"Whoa," Theo said, landing gracefully next to him. "You okay?"

Kade didn't reply. He marched to the nightstand and swiped a cigarette and the snake-flower lighter.

"I'll get you more blood," Theo tried.

Kade ignored him, flicking the lighter. It sputtered uselessly.

"One thing," Kade muttered, shaking with the injustice of it all. "Just—"

He cut himself off, swearing. Still sparks and no flame.

"Give me this *one* thing," he growled, flicking it faster and faster. "Come on, let me have this one! Bloody! *Thing!*"

He flicked it hard. One last spark, the barest hint of flame before it sputtered out.

"We can refill it," Theo started. "I can—"

Kade threw the lighter. It smashed into the lamp, which lurched sideways and tipped the entirety of their nightstand onto the floor. His strawberry needle caddy pinged across the room; cigarettes rolled under the bed.

"SHIT," Kade growled. The sound kept going, a wordless, guttural roar that made Sparky start scratching at the door. He launched himself at the bed, their useless bed that they used as a couch, and started ripping into it.

"Kade," Theo said. "*Hey!*"

Kade kept screaming, tearing the mattress apart. An inhuman, horrifying screech radiated from his throat. A few years ago, Kade would've been overjoyed to be able to make such a noise. He would've brought it out during homeroom, excited to watch his classmates duck and hide. Now it made him want to destroy everything in the room, especially the mirror.

He charged toward it, grabbing it off the dresser and

throwing it into the wall. Glass rained over the floor, bouncing into corners.

"What the hell?" Theo yelled.

Kade ignored him. This felt *good*. This felt like *doing something*. He couldn't help his friends and he couldn't stop this prophecy but he could always, *always* destroy something.

Next was the sewing machine. The stupid machine he spent so much time slaving over, making his dumb little clothes like he actually had a future in fashion. Like he had a future, *period*. Kade sped toward it, reaching out—

"Don't you dare!" Theo grabbed Kade's shoulders, holding him back. "Dude! You're freaking Sparky out!"

Kade stopped, panting. Ribbons of bedsheets dangled from his claws; glass powdered his hair. Sparky was clawing in earnest now, barking loudly.

Theo picked up the sewing machine, eyeing Kade warily. Then he headed to the door and blocked the doorway before opening it. So Sparky wouldn't come in and cut her paws, Kade realized as he watched Theo soothed her.

He looked around the ruined room, flooded with self-loathing. Ripping shit up, throwing things, screaming—who was he, his *dad*? He'd always told himself he wouldn't end up like him, and now Theo was petting Sparky and using that soft tone that Kade's mum always used with him after his dad's outbursts.

"Shit," Kade said shakily. He bent down, kneeling in the glass and patches of shredded duvet to search for the lighter he polished every night, even when Theo teased him for it.

"I'll clean this up," he blurted. "I'll—I'll fix it. Don't worry about it."

"Okay," Theo said after a second. He put the sewing machine down on the wrecked bed. He didn't look scared, at least. Just worried. He crouched down, stroking Sparky absentmindedly.

"It's under the bed," Theo said.

Kade looked up. "What?"

"The lighter." Theo pointed.

Kade bent down. Sure enough, there was his beloved lighter. Plus his strawberry needle caddy and a book he'd been missing for weeks.

"We're going about this the wrong way," Theo said as Kade retrieved the lighter. "We have to do *something*. We can't just sit here or we'll go crazy."

"Now he says it," Kade muttered. Then he winced. "I didn't mean that. I just—"

"It's okay." Theo stood, determined. "Want to go for a run suspiciously close to the Emmerson place?"

Kade opened his mouth to say yes.

Then he stopped.

Something was itching at the back of his head. Hard and pointed, like it wanted him to know. He *had* known, deep in a memory. He'd known it as he was dying, half in a dream. Then he'd forgotten it.

He took a deep breath, tasting fabric and glass and strange, charred florals.

"I think we need to go back to the flowers."

CHAPTER
NINETEEN

THE GREENHOUSE WAS GONE. Blackened struts stood up from the ground, the scent of melted plastic still hanging in the air days later.

The burned flowers stayed, too. Acrid and heavy, making Kade's eyes water.

"You grew them for me," he said. "The flowers. Victor did something to them, after. *Twisted* them for his own shit. But you grew them for me."

Theo didn't respond for a long time, turning over burned chunks of plastic with his foot.

"Okay," he said finally, looking like he would rather talk about anything else.

Kade rolled his eyes. "It's romantic!"

"It's two dudes who died centuries before we were born," Theo replied. "Do you feel anything?"

Kade considered. He stepped into the middle of the charred flowers, digging his sneakers into a patch of old blood. His own lifeblood pumping out of him and staining the dirt, the moss, the burned petals.

"Here," he said.

Theo twitched. He kept looking around like he was watching out for the Fletchers, but Kade knew that really, Theo didn't want to look at the spot where Kade died. Which Kade supposed was fair. It was bad enough going through it. He couldn't imagine what it must've been like carrying Kade's corpse to the car, not knowing if the vampirism process had worked.

Kade lay down. Part of him hoped for nothing, like all the times they'd trekked out to Cyth's tree to try and induce a vision. But the moment his head touched the burned ground, he was flooded with images: fire on meat. Worms in dirt. Flesh withering around the bone.

"Kade," Theo said, his voice very far away. "Are you—?"

"—even listening?"

Kade doesn't open his eyes. The moss is soft and nothing smells of blood. His head is on his beloved's lap, and they are both wearing gloves.

It is near the end, no matter how much Theo denies it.

"Kade," Theo says, low and persistent and lovely. "Kade!"

Kade wills himself closer to sleep. Just as he can feel its insistent call, the stiff corner of a newspaper presses gently into his chest.

Sleep falls even further away. Kade groans, forcing his eyes open.

Theo leans over him with a relieved smile. "Thought I lost you for a moment."

"Almost," Kade says, and yawns. "But no, your grating voice brought me back."

Theo smiles harder. "I was just reading about the plays showing in New York. Would you want to go to one, after we leave here?"

Kade sighs. Theo has been making more of an effort in these last months. Trying to convince Kade that they will have a life together after this. Kade does his best to believe it. But there is something stubborn in him, something a lot like his family line and a little like fate, that insists otherwise. A happy ending is a pretty idea. But Kade has never seen one in the flesh.

Then again, *he thinks, taking Theo's favorite curl and tugging.* All sorts of strange things exist in this world. Perhaps it isn't foolish to hope.

"I've never been to a play," Kade admits. "It would be nice."

"Perfect," Theo says. "I'll make a note. How do you feel about Shakespeare?"

"Men have died from time to time," Kade quotes. "And worms have eaten them, but not for love."

Theo laughs. "You know it better than me, evidently."

He runs a gloved finger over Kade's growing hair. His touch is gentle, and Kade pretends that he can have this forever. That they can have New York and plays and a story that doesn't end in tragedy.

"I was thinking about what you said," Theo said. "About

this clearing. Spring is coming up, it would be the perfect time for it. What do you think?"

"I think I want to sleep," Kade says, thinking of Shakespeare and worms and his mother reciting half remembered scripts as he fell asleep. "Do you mind? I managed two hours last night, at most."

Theo sits back against the tree, the newspaper rustling. "As you wish. As long as you come—"

"—back to me."

Kade's eyes fluttered behind his lids. Theo had been so clear before. Now he sounded like he was shouting from the wrong end of a very long tunnel.

"Kade," Theo said, too far now. Kade could barely hear him over the roar of flames. Over bones snapping, petals crisping. Dirt showering down. They had done this all before and here it was, coming around—

—again it will happen again everything has already happened the flowers grow and die and rot and come back next year dirt in a hole bones in a hole flesh rots flowers rot the hunters curl them together touching in death as they couldn't in life one final kindness one last apology before they cover them with—

—dirt stained Theo's beautiful hair, his worried face haloed by moonlight.

Theo was saying something. Kade couldn't hear it. Half of him was still stuck in the visions, the memories, the *roots*. Thick and dark and deep in the ground underneath, feasting.

Finally, Theo's voice filtered through, thick and murky, as if through a fog.

"Kade," he said desperately. "You have to come back now. Okay? Come back to me."

He squeezed Kade's arms.

I've been thrashing, Kade realized dully. Burned petal fragments stuck in Theo's hair from where Kade had been writhing in the earth, flinging up bits of soil and moss.

"Hey," Theo said, face collapsing with relief. "Are you with me?"

Kade reached up to pick the burned fragment out of Theo's curls. All these pink petals that Theo had cultivated for him. So beautiful. So *hungry*.

"We fed them," Kade mumbled.

Theo's relief faltered. "What?"

Kade grabbed his shirt, fingers locking shakily in the dirt-streaked fabric. "It's us. We're *here*."

"We are here," Theo said, half confused, half soothing. "We're okay."

Kade shook his head, rot still heavy in his nostrils. Burned flesh and dirt and his own blood baked to the ground underneath him. He shuddered, wiping furiously at his clothes, trying to get it off.

"No," he spat, wiping desperately at the moss

sticking to the back of his hair. "*We*. Past us. They buried us here, together. Under the flowers."

Theo stilled. He looked down at the burned petals they were crouched in, swallowing against a dry throat as the horror set in.

Kade panted. He could still see it, see *them*: bare fingers interlaced between their bodies. Together in death.

Dread filled him in a horrifying wave, as real and solid as the moss sticking to his cheek. "We're doomed," he whispered "Oh, shit. We're *so* bloody doomed."

Theo knelt over him: twisted mirrors of the bones that lay underneath the earth.

"We're not doomed," he insisted. "We—the other boys, they had nothing to do with us. They're just something that happened a long time ago."

Kade laughed wetly. Of course Theo would believe that. He hadn't lived his whole life with the same stories repeating behind and ahead, stories his family knew by heart and still acted sad about when they came to pass. He'd tried so hard to escape it and yet here he was: throwing something he loved around his bedroom. Breaking mirrors. Screaming so loud it scared the dog. The same story over and over.

If they sabotaged the ritual, Victor would just kill them. Bring them back in another two hundred years. They'd do this again. Kade shuddered, picturing it: bones buried on top of bones, two boys with their faces and personalities and loves crouched in the very place they were crouched now, having the same horrifying realization.

"We need to get out," Kade whispered.

"Kade," Theo started.

Kade cut him off. "Let's get out of here. We can...we can leave town, take Sundance and Sparky, we can just *go*. We can hide, he won't find us—"

"He will," Theo said quietly. "Kade. Sweetheart—"

"Don't *sweetheart* me," Kade cried. A black tear tracked down his cheek and soaked into the dirt. "How do you not *get* this? We're *doomed*. We were doomed before either of us even *existed*. You and me, sunshine, we're punctuation points at the end of a tragedy. We did this already, we're dead, we're *bones*—"

"Kade," Theo said, voice breaking.

His phone rang, so sudden and shrill that they both jumped. Kade actually flew a little, hovering over the destroyed earth before slamming back down.

Theo wiped his face and fumbled his phone out of his pocket. "It's Liss."

Kade grabbed for the phone, but Theo was already turning it toward him, the screen glowing furiously in the dark:

ok, u can come now.

Police lights made the whole street bleed red and blue. There were four cop cars pulled up outside the

Emmerson place, the parents huddled together on the lawn as police questioned them. They looked dazed. They had woodchips and plaster in their hair.

"An animal," Kade heard the mom say as they cruised past with the window down. She spoke too fast for it to be anything but lying. "It was...*huge*."

A few houses down, Beverly and Felicity stood next to their car. A cop was walking away from them, looking troubled.

Theo pulled over ahead of them and paused. "Don't get out of the car."

"I'm fine," Kade insisted. But he held his breath, all the Sloans' tiny cuts and bruises making his mouth water. Beverly held her arm strangely, her jaw set in a tight mask of pain and deep annoyance as she tried to dab peroxide into her daughter's split lip.

Felicity batted her away.

"Heeey," Kade heard her crow as Theo walked up. "You made it!"

Then she grinned, her broken-bone smile so huge and brittle it could only mean one thing.

CHAPTER
TWENTY

FOR THE THIRD time in two weeks, Principal Kelly called an assembly.

"I'm sure you've all heard by now that Ryan Emmerson has gone missing," he began, which Theo thought was a strange way to put it. *Delilah* Emmerson had gone missing. *Ryan* Emmerson had been stolen out of their goddamn house by an ancient vampire. And they weren't the only thing Victor stole.

It broke into some old hunting shit, Felicity had told them last night, her mother holding her still to wipe the blood off her eyebrow. *Family hadn't looked at it for decades. But he was holding a dress when he dragged Ryan away. White and flowy, like in the book.*

"And I'm sure you know that it is official: we have an animal terrorizing our streets," Principal Kelly continued. "Witnesses described it as very large and potentially winged—"

"Holy shit," called someone from the crowd. "It's a real-life vampire!"

"It's mothman," another guy yelled.

A wave of laughter swept over the hall.

Theo looked at Kade, who was standing uncannily still beside him. It was the sort of joke that would make Kade hide a smile. But his face was blank, gaze aimed straight ahead. Listening to the whispers, Theo realized. Even though Theo had warned him not to. He'd already caught a few nervous barks aimed at Kade as they filed into the hall. Theo had to stop himself from growling back. Not just out of indignation—they still didn't know if Kade was safe to be here. If he could hold himself back.

Principal Kelly glared out as the hall fell silent. "Your classmate is *dead*. Others are missing. This is no time for jokes." He cleared his throat and stood back from the microphone. "Alrighty. Finn Harley has kindly volunteered to pass on some valuable information about staying safe in these difficult times."

Kade finally looked over. *What the hell,* he mouthed.

Theo nodded, watching incredulously as Finn strode out onstage, glowing with smug excitement. He looked like how Kade used to describe himself during his brief phase as a child magician: he had something up his sleeve that he was too excited to hide.

"Alright folks," Finn said, leaning into the microphone so close it let out a burst of feedback.

Everyone winced. No one more than Theo and

Kade, both of whom had to bite back twin yelps of pain.

"Asshole," Kade hissed.

"Got that right," Theo muttered.

Finn leaned back with a nervous laugh. "Sorry! Anyway, let's get this show on the road. There's a monster on the loose!"

Theo watched his classmates trade looks. Everybody had heard about the description Mr. Emmerson had given before immediately taking it back—*it was taller than any of us, and it had wings.* Nobody had mentioned wings after that, it sounded too ridiculous. But Lock was a small town. Word got around. However much the officials wanted to use the word *animal*, everybody was whispering about monsters. About the sudden spike in dead animals in the woods. About Skeeter and Victor Fairgood, their bodies ripped apart and left to rot.

"If you find yourself at the monster's door," Finn continued. "Get out your pepper spray and your pocketknife. Blind the bastard, then stab him in the throat!"

"Okay," Principal Kelly said, stepping up. "That isn't what we discussed."

"Joking! I'm joking, sir." Finn flashed him a smile, reaching like he was going to straighten the man's tie before chickening out and flicking his collar instead.

"But seriously," Finn said, turning back to the audience. "This is some real sh—I mean, stuff. Use the buddy system! Don't let your friends out of your sight!

If you have no friends, grab the other friendless losers—I mean, people—and team up. Strangers in numbers! Divided we fall, Lockians! Stay safe out there."

He paused, glancing back at the principal. Theo waited for whatever clumsy shit he'd been hiding up his sleeve to come out. He was too far to quit now.

"And remember," Finn said, so close to the microphone that it spat out another hiss of static and made everyone flinch again. "My birthday party is in TWO DAYS, and if you want to break out your wings and fangs—"

Principal Kelly surged up and twisted the microphone away.

"We're picking winners," Finn yelled. "Best costume gets a mystery prize!"

He ducked away from a security guard who was advancing onto the stage, but not before rummaging in the podium and pulling out a vampire mask. He shoved it on, letting out a pathetic screech before running offstage.

"Well," Principal Kelly said into the chorus of murmurs breaking out through the room. "That was... deeply indecent."

Theo didn't listen to the rest. The hall was too loud, a cacophony of hushed anxiety and shock and genuine laughter. There was someone trying not to cry in the back of the hall, muffling their sobs.

A senior turned to shoot a snarl at Kade, teeth bared. "Guess we better get our pepper spray, Monster."

Kade twitched. His lips peeled back.

"Don't," Theo whispered.

Kade glared at him. He looked exhausted, even though they'd been out hunting last night. Two more deer gone. They were running out fast, and still Kade wasn't satisfied.

The rest of the talk passed without incident. Theo stuck by Kade's side as they filed out of the hall, picking out Principal Kelly's angry comment above the rest, muttered to a substitute teacher: "Whose bright idea was it to let that little shit onstage?"

Theo caught up with Kade as they set up the dodgeball line.

"Are you sure you're okay to be here? We have two days, you can stay home—"

"I'm fine," Kade said darkly. "Until Saturday, anyway."

Theo sighed. "Kade."

Kade whirled on him, his eyes flickering black. "He has everything he needs, Theo! He got the dress from the Emmerson house, which means the bag Finn dragged up obviously had the spear! We're *fucked*!"

"Hey," called Mr. Wellerman, the timid teacher who reluctantly took over after Coach Cheech's mysterious disappearance. "No swearing, Renfield. Please don't make me send you to Principal Kelly's office."

"I wish you would," Kade growled. He slurred the last word, his teeth sharpening.

Theo tugged him away. "*Hey*. You said you were fine."

"I *am* fine," Kade insisted, pulling his sleeve out of Theo's grip. He was wearing his gym uniform, his baggy shirt and tiny shorts showing more pale skin than Theo had seen on Kade since summer.

Theo pulled his gaze away from Kade's wiry thighs and focused on the dodgeball team lining up on the other side of the orange cones.

"Okay," Mr. Wellerman called, brandishing his whistle. "And...play ball!"

Kade surged for the closest ball. Theo held back a sigh as he watched him pace down the cones, lobbing dodgeballs with such ferocity that people fell under their force. Only a minute into the game and half the team was out, everyone staring at Kade in amazement.

"Kade," Theo said warningly.

"I know," Kade insisted. He picked up another dodgeball, the plastic straining under his fingers. He scanned the other team, and Theo winced as everyone scrambled not to be his next target. This was the first time Kade had put any effort into gym class, and absolutely no one was enjoying it.

Twenty more minutes and they could break for lunch. Kade had a thermos of deer blood in his locker that could tide him over until the end of the day. If he just held out until then—

Kade hurled another dodgeball. Everyone on the other team ducked. Even a few of their own team ducked as the ball hurtled through the air, landing in Oscar Alvarez's stomach hard enough to make him fall to his knees.

Theo tugged on Kade's shirt. "Okay. You're done."

Kade wrenched his shirt from his grip. "I'm *fine!*"

"People are *looking,*" Theo reminded him.

"God forbid," Kade sneered, stepping up so close their noses almost brushed. "Still afraid of me embarrassing you, golden boy?"

Theo blinked. It had been a while since Kade called him that. It had been a while since *anyone* called him that.

"I don't care what people think," Theo said lowly. "As long as they don't think *certain things* that they *really* shouldn't know, especially not after today's assembly—"

"Hey," came a wheezy voice from beyond the cone line.

Theo turned.

Oscar Alvarez was limping toward them, a hand curled over his stomach. Theo wouldn't be surprised if it bruised. Oscar always bruised easily. He had an inhaler and chronic nosebleeds and some blood condition Theo couldn't remember the name of. Or maybe a bone condition—he was always showing up with a new cast. Back in the day people called him Spongebob Boy, quoting that one line about glass bones and paper skin.

"That was messed up," Oscar croaked. "Whatever

fight you're having with your boyfriend, don't take it out on us, man."

Kade went dangerously still. He stared at Oscar with eyes that Theo knew very well: predator eyes. The last thing that deer saw before he lunged.

The scent of iron hit him. Theo's gaze dropped to Oscar's nose, where a thick drop of blood was rolling toward his painted upper lip.

"Kade," Theo warned.

Kade snarled and sprung.

Theo slammed into him, but it was too late: Kade dragged them both down on top of Oscar, who was hollering before they even hit the ground.

"Don't," Theo said, locking his arms around Kade's torso. "Kade, holy shit, stop—"

Kade hissed and spat, struggling to close the distance. Oscar had his arms up over his face, shrieking for Mr. Wellerman to intervene.

Mr. Wellerman did not intervene. He did, however, stand on the sidelines yelling for Kade and Theo to stop.

"I'm *trying*," Theo gritted, trying to calculate a way of grabbing Kade that wouldn't burn him. He couldn't hook his arms around Kade's neck. Couldn't even grab his shoulders. He was stuck with his arms locked around Kade's torso, cursing whoever decided that gym should happen in a skimpy shirt and shorts.

Their classmates crowded a safe distance away. Some of them were barking. Others were silent, still wary of

Kade's killer aim. One boy started howling until his friend, who Theo had seen sharing manga at Ryan Emmerson's cafeteria table, nudged him to stop.

Theo lowered his mouth as close to Kade's head as he dared. "*Kade*. This hunger, it's not you. You don't belong to it. You belong to *me*."

Kade stopped trying to buck Theo off. He was still growling, a low thing that rumbled deep in his throat. His eyes flickered: black, gray, black. Thank god Oscar had his arms over his face and no one else was close enough to see.

"That's it," Theo coaxed. "Come back to me. Right now."

Kade stopped growling. Theo almost didn't notice—their barking classmates were getting louder.

Kade shuddered and pushed himself up, staggering. Theo grabbed the back of his shirt to steady him.

"'M fine," Kade mumbled, squeezing his eyes shut. "I'm...I'm good. I'm fine."

Several of their classmates bent down to help Oscar Alvarez off the floor. He was still trembling, blood dripping down his neck. He was a quiet kid, never joining in on the bullying or barking. He'd never been in a fight before. Theo bet he'd never seen someone so vicious until Kade was on top of him, teeth bared.

"Sorry," Kade slurred. "Oscar. Sorry."

Mr. Wellerman approached them, a clipboard held in front of him like a shield.

"You two," he said, sounding deeply relieved he didn't have to get involved. "Principal's office. Now."

"On it," Theo said. He pulled Kade away. Kade's gaze stuck on Oscar's bloody makeup all the way out of the gym.

Theo marched him to the disabled bathroom and locked the door.

"It's okay," he told Kade. "Hey. Nobody got hurt. How are you feeling?"

Kade laughed wetly.

"I'm fine," he croaked. "I'm fine. I'm *good*. I'm…"

His lip trembled. Theo watched him pull it into a snarl, try to make himself become the guy everyone was afraid of. For a second it even stuck, his new vampire instincts kicking in. Then his whole face crumpled.

He dropped to the floor, burying his head in his knees.

Theo followed, squeezing his shorts-clad thigh. "Kade."

"I'm a monster," Kade blurted, black tears spilling down his cheeks. "Shit. I wanted to stop giving reasons for people to call me a monster, and then I go and do *that*. I bit the crap out of Felicity, you have to tackle me every hunt so I don't go crazy and run out into the road and chase down a minivan. Why is it so hard? Everybody was right about me. I really am a monster. I'm a monster and I'm doomed—"

"Stop it." Theo grabbed his shirt, wishing more than ever that they were wearing gloves. Theo would give anything to touch his face right now, to make Kade focus those big gray eyes on him. "That's not true."

Kade shoved his hands off. "Don't pull that shit, man. I've known it since I was born, even *before* that. I'm a monster and I'm going to die on Saturday, and everyone out there is going to cheer! Ding-dong, Monster's dead—"

"They don't know you!" Theo yelled. "Not like I do. I've been trapped with you for a while, and I know you're good and kind and...and sweet, you're *so* stupidly sweet under all your goddamn spikes."

He rubbed Kade's gym shirt, the ache to touch him throbbing like a heartbeat.

"And I know that I love you," he continued.

Kade's face collapsed again. "Theo—"

"You're going to make clothes and I'm gonna—I don't know, forage. Cook. Be a landscaper. Whatever we do, we'll do it together." Theo bent down and kissed Kade's gym shirt, right over his heart. "Just two more nights, baby. Everything's gonna be fine. Okay?"

Kade snorted, wiping his black-streaked cheeks. He still didn't believe, Theo could tell. But he would lie, for him.

"Okay," Kade whispered.

SOMETHING WAS ROTTING in Milly's house.

It was in the very first stages of decay, but Theo could smell it when he walked into the living room: sweet and cloying, overpowering the scent of old coffee and dust.

Kade wrinkled his nose. So quietly only Theo could hear it, he muttered: "Super smelling is *not* as fun as you promised."

"I don't remember promising that," Theo replied. He sniffed again. He was pretty sure the smell was coming from the coffee table covered with old dishes and older books. Milly had obviously been busy; the whiteboard was covered in new string. His mother's picture had been moved to the center in a way that made Theo nervous. Did his mom have a role in the ritual after all?

"Milly," Kade called. "There's something fermenting under your stack of mugs..."

He trailed off. Russel emerged from the kitchen, carrying a bottle of store-brand lemonade.

Kade shot Theo a look. He'd been betting Russel wouldn't come. Theo's text was pretty last-minute, and Russel hadn't replied. But here he was, clearing a spot on the coffee table for the bottle of lemonade.

"I got it," he said. He thunked the lemonade down and picked up the stack of mugs with a well-concealed grimace. "How are you two feeling?"

Theo looked at Kade as they sat down on the couch. He felt worried about his boyfriend—and now, about what Milly was going to tell him about his mom. He felt annoyed he still had to do homework when he was trying to stop the town from getting destroyed. He was torn in two about the prospect of fighting his parents tomorrow. And of course, he was endlessly in agony over not being able to touch the love of his life. Or love of his death, as Kade had pointed out last night. He'd even sewn it into a shirt, complete with red glittery sequins.

"Eager to get this over with," Theo replied. "Where's Milly?"

"There's a cat having trouble. Milly went to check on it." Russel headed back into the kitchen with the stack of plates and mugs, calling: "Where are the others?"

"Sundance is coming from work. Felicity said they're

going to be late," Kade said. "They're finding a new disguise for Skeeter. She tore the big hat in a fit of rage after losing a game of Connect Four."

"I'll grab some glasses anyway," Russel called from the kitchen. The kitchen tap started running. "Theo, could you help me out?"

"Sure," Theo called back. He flexed his hands anxiously. Something in Russel's tone told him he wasn't going in there to help with dishes.

Kade lowered his voice. "Need more hands?"

Still annoyed. Still hungry. But he knew where Theo's mind was at.

Theo shook his head. He squeezed Kade's gloved pinkie and headed to the kitchen, knowing Kade would be listening in anyway.

Russel was standing at the tiny sink, rinsing Milly's dirty plates. He made a face as mold and rotted grapes clumped down the drain.

"She gets a little distracted when she's deep in this," Theo explained, taking a plate from the drying rack and rubbing it with a dish towel. "She was back to normal in winter, but this past month she's basically gone underground. The bookstore's closed this week. For all the good it's done us."

"She's very dedicated," Russel said lightly.

Theo grunted an agreement. She *was* dedicated. Without her they would still have no idea what the prophecy said or what the Fletchers were trying to do. But he wanted her to give them a *way out*, dammit.

Something to derail tomorrow's ritual before it came. He wanted a spell, easy and fast. He wanted a happy ending.

Russel brushed the last of the rotting grapes down the drain, and the smell of decay went with it.

"There we go," Russel muttered. He took a deep breath. Theo tensed, tightening his fingers dangerously around the plate he was drying.

"I never really said, after..." Russel sighed. "I'm so sorry about your dad."

Theo swallowed hard, eyes on the plate. It was already dry, but he kept rubbing.

"You did say it," he offered.

"But not after I found out what really happened." Russel went rigid, as if waiting for his bones to start churning inside of him. When it didn't happen, he continued: "I...I can't imagine how this feels, Theo. You deserved so much better."

Theo gave him a tight smile. He didn't want to talk about his dad. He *had* to, because of the ritual tomorrow, but that was talk about the evil vampire using Theo and Kade for his selfish gains. Not about Theo's *dad*, who drove him to basketball games and took him hiking on weekends and taught him how to shave and was going to try and make Theo murder his boyfriend tomorrow.

He grabbed another plate, pretending to examine a nonexistent speck of grime.

"It's more than that," Russel continued, drying his

scarred hands on his shorts. "I'm sorry I wasn't there for you."

"Russel—"

"No, come on, let me say it." Russel hesitated. "I was an idiot. With the—"

He motioned wordlessly at his mouth, indicating the silence spell with an embarrassed wince. Then he replaced it with that soft expression that Theo shied away from instinctively.

Russel sighed. "You're a good person, Theo. Your parents tried to kill your heart. And you didn't let that happen. I'm...I'm so proud of you. And I'm *so* goddamn sorry."

Theo nodded stiffly. The plate creaked in his grip. He couldn't let go of it and he couldn't look up, couldn't see Russel look at him with such horrible tenderness. It made Theo's skin crawl. It made him want to hug him. To argue that he *had* been there for Theo, he'd been there for years, cheering him up after his parents yelled at him and teaching him how to treat stinging nettle. What to do after stamping through a patch of poison ivy. How to trim a rose without getting cut. Once Theo nicked him with a pair of garden shears and he wasn't even mad, just chuckled and held his hand over an exposed root. He'd smiled over at Theo as blood dripped down his wrist.

It's okay, he'd said. *I'm feeding it. Look, it's growing more petals already.*

"Theo," Russel said gently. He touched Theo's shoulder.

Theo cracked the plate he was holding.

Russel jumped. He stared down at the broken plate, split down the middle.

"Sorry," Theo started. "I—"

A car alarm went off.

Russel sighed. "That's my damn car. I'll be back in a minute."

Theo nodded numbly, stepping out of the way for Russel to get to the back door. The alarm blared even louder for a second, then the back door slammed and the sound returned to a tolerable shriek.

Theo piled the broken halves into the trash and headed back into the living room. He'd buy Milly a new plate later.

Kade was perched on the edge of the couch. He had his hands over his ears, wincing with each whine of the alarm. "It's like getting hit with a pickax," he grumbled as Theo joined him.

Theo nodded, brushing shards of ceramic off his palms. They landed on the floor with the rest of the mess. Next week, Theo would come over and help Milly clear all of this up. There would be no reason to look into this anymore. No more ritual looming over them. No more missing classmates. No more evil plots to unveil. Just school and a minimum wage job and community college applications in whatever city Kade took him to.

"Theo," Kade prompted. He tugged Theo toward the living room.

The middle of the clue board had been cleared. Huge letters loomed across the top of it: RITUAL NIGHT, with a sketch of Finn Harley's house, and everybody's pictures gathered around.

Theo reached up to touch a yearbook photo of Skeeter, grimacing and heavy with braces. Milly had doodled a cartoon crossbow next to her. Next to most of them, now that Theo looked closely.

"We have enough of us to cover all the exits," he said. "Right? I've been to his house, it's not *that* big."

Kade sighed. "So what, we just loiter around until whatever they're planning happens and then we deal with the fallout?"

"I guess. I just don't know how it's gonna connect up to—"

The car alarm stopped.

Kade tensed. It was so sudden and complete that Theo tensed with him, ready to throw himself on top of him to stop him from lunging at Milly, fangs bared. But then Kade snapped his head toward him, eyes huge and gray, no black to be seen.

Theo opened his mouth to ask what was wrong. Then he heard it: footsteps. Heavy and urgent, lurching up the porch.

The front door slammed open. Theo and Kade surged up from the couch just in time to see Skeeter in a pink ski mask, holding up Beverly Sloan by her armpits. Beverly was stumbling, blood matting her dark hair.

Theo grabbed Kade's sleeve.

"I'm fine," Kade managed, hands clenched tight at his sides.

"Sons of bitches," Beverly slurred. She stunk of blood, a thick river streaming from the back of her head. She wobbled, pulled herself out of Skeeter's arms, and braced herself in the living room doorway.

"Whoa," Skeeter said. "Um, Beverly—"

She reached for her. Beverly jerked away and stretched an arm toward Theo.

Theo blurred forward to catch her before she toppled over. She gripped his elbows hard enough to bruise a human, face twisted in a desperate snarl.

"Felicity," she mumbled. "*Felicity*."

"They knocked her out," Skeeter said. "I...I was in the woods, I didn't hear until it was too late. I'm sorry. I tried to heal her, but she kept saying to drive—"

Beverly tightened her grip on Theo's arms. One of her pupils was bigger than the other. Theo was flooded with fear, remembering the awful sound of Mr. Fletcher's insides twisting as the spell took hold.

"Don't say anything else," he reminded her, placing his fingers on her temples.

"I *know*," she snapped, her voice clumsy and wet.

Theo concentrated. There was a sickening *click* as her cracked skull popped back into place, the skin creeping over it.

"Theo," Kade said, strained.

Theo grunted. Bone to seal, skin to regrow. Skeeter bent down beside him, face pinched as she held her breath against the heavy scent of blood. She touched the nape of Beverly's neck, and suddenly the bone was smooth and the skin was regrowing a lot faster.

"*Theo*," Kade repeated.

"Go into the other room," Theo replied. "I'm almost done."

Kade stepped into view. His eyes flickered black, hands shaking with the effort of not looking at the bloody Beverly Sloan.

"Car alarm," he said.

Theo didn't pay much attention to Skeeter's low gasp. He was too busy watching Beverly's skin seal crawl over white bone.

"What? Yeah, it's stopped."

Kade nodded stiffly, white-knuckling his phone. "Where's Russel?"

The driver's window was smashed. Blood dripped down the glass. There was a note tucked under the windshield wipers in the same handwriting that once signed Theo's permission slips:

Until tomorrow.

Theo crushed it in his fist and turned back to Kade. "Anything from Sundance?"

"No," Kade said, voice breaking as he held the

phone up to his ear again. "She's not...she's not answering."

"She's probably driving," Theo tried. "She'll show up any minute."

Kade nodded. But Theo could see it in his face: he didn't believe him. Which was fair. Theo didn't believe himself either.

The call timed out. Kade cursed, wiping his face.

"Try again," Theo said.

Kade did.

The call timed out.

CHAPTER
TWENTY-TWO

KADE STARED at the outfit lying on his bed.

A black, flowy shirt with a bright red cravat. Tight pants with bleeding hearts embroidered in the pockets. An ornate Colombina face mask, as blue as the bottom of a lake. And to top it all off: an honest-to-god silk cape.

This outfit screamed drama, secrets, *trouble*. The kind of clothes a vampire would wear for the most important night of his life.

Kade sighed longingly and looked down at the ripped jeans and ratty T-shirt he was wearing.

U STAY SOFT / U GET EATEN, the old shirt declared. It needed mending. The *O* was wearing away yet again.

Sparky scratched at his bedroom door. Kade turned, but it was already swinging open.

"How do I look?" Theo asked, adjusting his gloves. "Not very monstery. But party-ready?"

Theo was beautiful. Devastatingly so. He was wearing the shirt Kade had made for his birthday: a simple white dress shirt tailored to fit Theo perfectly. Embroidered tendrils of green coiled around the collar, forming ferns.

Theo grabbed two cigarettes from their bedside table. "Just so you know, I'm going to take your stunned silence as a compliment."

Kade nodded mutely. Theo had been extra upbeat today, clattering around the house like he was trying to distract Kade from the gaping maw Sundance left behind. As far as they could tell, one of Theo's parents had grabbed her the night before, while she was walking to her car after work. Her matching blue mask sat on the sewing table with all the others Kade had brought last week, before Felicity, Milly, and Russel went missing. Half their group had been taken in one damn night.

Sparky nosed at Kade's hand. He glanced down at her adoring, worried gaze. There was love there. He'd never doubted it. Even before he knew Theo loved him, he knew Sparky would die for him. If she wasn't being mind-controlled by her maker, at least.

"Sorry you can't come," he told her.

Sparky whined.

Theo touched her head, inches away from Kade's fingers. "I know, girl. You've been doing better when we train. But you kicked my ass last time Victor was around, and your training hasn't been going great. We can't risk that tonight. You're on laundry room duty."

Sparky whined louder.

"Go on," Theo said, opening the bedroom door. "We'll be back later. Promise."

Sparky slunk out the door, turning to give them one last baleful look before Theo shut it behind her.

Theo held out the second cigarette, still unlit. Kade leaned in, letting Theo slot it gently into his mouth. Theo stepped closer, pressing the flaring tip of his cigarette to Kade's.

For a second the only sound was their breathing. It filled the room, which was suddenly smaller with Theo standing so close, watching him so intently. They breathed out at the same time, smoke mingling between them, and Kade shivered. Their past selves didn't smoke. They never got to have this. Their past selves didn't get to have a lot of things.

Kade tore himself away from Theo's gaze and picked up his mask from the bed. "Where's yours?"

"In the car."

Kade nodded, tying his mask in place with the dark blue ribbons. "Alright. Let's go."

"Whoa, hey." Theo caught his arm, the buttery leather of his glove soft on Kade's elbow. "Forgetting something?"

He motioned down at the clothes Kade had spent all week making.

Kade sighed. "I don't want to tempt fate."

Theo stared at him, uncomprehending.

"It's exactly what a doomed teenage vampire would wear when he's about to die tragically with his boyfriend," Kade explained. "If I wear it, I'm just playing into the narrative. If I wear casual..." He plucked at his faded shirt. "Less of a story moment."

Theo tried not to smile, smoke curling around his twitching mouth. His gloved fingers tugged at Kade's shirt, right in the spot Kade had just been touching. Over the damaged O in *SOFT*.

"Well," he said quietly. "You look good."

"Yeah, yeah." Kade swallowed. He couldn't meet Theo's eyes when he was being all sweet and sincere like this. He chewed his lip, which would never be chapped again. Then he paused.

Theo was still holding his shirt.

Kade looked up.

Theo's smile was gone. His grip on Kade's shirt was so tight his gloves creaked.

"Whoa, hey." Kade stubbed their cigarettes on the carpet, and it was telling that Theo didn't even complain. "What's wrong?"

Theo laughed. It was, Kade figured, a pretty stupid question to ask a teenager on the night of the horrifying ritual his parents had been planning since before he was born.

"Other than the obvious?" Theo cupped Kade's face, stroking leather over the edges of his mask. "I miss your blush. I miss your smell, you smell different now. I can't believe—I can't *believe* I killed you and I *still* can't touch you."

"You are touching me," Kade whispered. Not for the first time, he wished he had the burn scars back. The one on his hand, he could live without. The kiss scar on his neck...he'd mourn *that* for the rest of his existence.

Theo shook his head. "I want to touch all of you!"

Kade's breath hitched.

"Not even—" Theo sighed, looking away like he always did whenever that topic came up. "I just want to hold you. I want to kiss you properly, you *deserve* a first kiss."

The longing in Theo's eyes made Kade squirm. He wanted to find a dark hole to hide in. He wanted to throw himself into Theo's arms, burns be damned. He wanted, he *wanted*, he'd been wanting so *long*. Wrapped up in Theo's arms at night, a sheet between them. Theo's gloved finger in his belt loop in the school halls, pulling him close. The closest they ever came was Theo kissing his neck before a bite. And Kade could never enjoy it like he wanted, the agony chasing out the pleasure before it had a chance to settle.

Theo started to pull away.

Kade caught him by his embroidered collar.

"We can't kiss," he said slowly, thumbing at the fern he'd sewn into the fabric. "But..."

"But?" Theo frowned. "Kade, what's happening?"

Kade thought about dropping it. They had a party to get to. Friends and aunts to save. The night lay out in front of them, a terrible darkness with vague shapes moving in the distance. Kade didn't know if he'd ever get this chance again.

"This might be the last time we see each other," Kade said in a rush. "Unless Victor brings us back in another hundred years, I don't know. So I was...I was wondering. Do you want...?"

Hands shaking, he touched Theo's belt.

Theo blinked, all want and regret. "Kade. We can't."

"We can," Kade blurted. "Sort of. Not *properly*, but we can do...things. As long as we don't go skin to skin."

He cringed, closing his eyes. He couldn't help it. He felt like he had peeled himself down to raw nerves, waiting to see what Theo would do with them.

Theo didn't speak for several mortifying seconds. Kade's mind whirred with a hundred horrifying responses, none of them sounding anything like:

"I know."

"You *know*?" Kade's eyes flew open. Theo was watching him, blond brows furrowed.

"Sure," Theo said. "Had a lot of time to think while you were sleeping. My mind wandered."

He smiled, embarrassed. But there was something else in his expression, something that made Kade surge forward and bury his masked face against Theo's shoulder, wrap his arms around Theo's waist.

Theo hesitated. Then he lifted his arms to hold Kade tight. Keeping his head up, so his chin didn't accidentally press into Kade's cheek.

"Why didn't you say anything?" Kade mumbled.

Theo rubbed his back. "It's not that I don't want to. I *really* want. But we have, like, twenty minutes—"

"Not a problem."

Theo laughed. His arms tightened around Kade, ducking to whisper in his ear. "I'd forget myself. I'd try to kiss you, or—or touch you, and I can't heal you anymore. So no."

Kade nodded. His throat was thick, bitterness clogging his throat.

"Right. Yeah." He pulled back, putting some sensible distance between them. "Honestly, probably good you said no. It'd just tempt the narrative."

Theo caught him before he could get too far. He dragged him back in, pressing a careful kiss to Kade's mask.

"We'll be okay," Theo said. "Tomorrow, we can do whatever we want. Tonight..."

He trailed off, the apprehension he was trying to hide finally shining through. They'd spent a year waiting for this. Depending on who you asked, they'd been waiting their whole lives.

Depending on who you asked, they'd been waiting even longer than that.

The Harley house was full of monsters.

Unfortunately, Lock only had one party supplies store within a four-hour radius. Kade counted four

Frankensteins, six ghosts, and eight slutty witches in the exact same dress. And, of course, dozens of vampires. Everybody wore the same variation of masquerade masks available at the Party City three towns over. There was so much fake blood Kade's mouth watered.

"Felicity's going to be so pissed she didn't get to be the sluttiest witch," he told Theo, desperate for something that would make him feel less doomed. "Her outfit would've made all of these girls look like shit."

Theo didn't laugh like he'd hoped. He was scanning the dark living room, eyes darting from face to face. Searching for Finn.

A pointed whisper reached his ears. "Do you boys see anyone?"

Kade started to jerk toward the voice.

"Subtle," Theo reminded him, too quiet for human ears.

Kade's gaze roamed totally casually over Beverly Sloan, who was positioned down the hall at the main entrance. She was wearing an over-the-top ballgown to hide the array of weapons underneath it, and she glared witheringly at anyone who tried to talk to her. It was so effective that no one called her out on it.

Kade shook his head. Her lips thinned, and Kade heard her swear.

Skeeter had the back entrance. She and Beverly both wore the matching blue masks Kade gave them. At any other time Kade would find that deeply cool, like they were a crew of thieves about to undergo a heist.

But he couldn't stop thinking about the unused masks sitting on his sewing table.

"Not like Finn to be late to his own party," Theo said, looking around the cavernous living room full of their masked classmates.

"Maybe he's feeling shy," Kade suggested. "Or hey, maybe he had a change of heart. Maybe he decided vampire powers aren't worth killing his classmates over and he's told your parents to shove it."

Theo didn't answer. He was still watching faces: devils and ghouls and murder victims and a never-ending stream of vampires; lights flashing purple and red over the room. They even had a smoke machine.

Kade tugged his sleeve. "Dance with me."

Theo frowned. "What?"

"Dance with me," Kade repeated. He tried to smile. "We can watch the crowd without looking like total weirdos."

Kade waited for Theo to say something like, *since when do you care about looking like a weirdo?* But Theo's intense gaze softened, and he slid his gloved hands around Kade's waist.

Kade pressed his mouth into Theo's shoulder with a shaky sigh. He'd spent so much time wanting to be special, wanting a *story*—and now he was smack-dab in the middle of one and all he wanted was to dance with his boyfriend at a party. How the tables turned.

He clutched Theo tightly, hoping against hope that this wasn't the last time. He wanted a lifetime of dances with this boy. More than one lifetime, if possible.

Theo's confused voice pulled him out of his yearning.

"Does everyone seem…" Theo wrinkled his nose. "*Really* wasted? The party just started."

Kade looked up. His classmates did seem more drunk than they should have been. He counted several of them stumbling around, even slurring. A sophomore bumped into them, and Kade caught the distinct stench of hard liquor on his breath.

"God, it's like paint thinner," Theo complained.

Kade nodded. "Maybe Finn has a stash. Or—"

Before he could finish, his eyes caught on a pale face in the crowd. It was tense and urgent, pushing through the throng toward them.

Kade swallowed, curling his fingers reflexively around Theo's arms. "Incoming."

Theo twisted to look. Then he dropped Kade's waist and stepped in front of him, raising his arm protectively.

But Aaron barely looked at Kade as he came to a stop in front of them. He was panting, limp hair flopping in his eyes. He was wearing cargo pants and a duffel bag strapped to his back. Unlike their stumbling classmates, there was no trace of liquor on his breath. His eyes were clear and panicked.

"Hey," Aaron snapped. "Where's Liss? Her mom's

here but she won't talk to me. Even though she's one of the only ones who *can* talk to me!"

Kade looked at Theo. Theo looked at him, jaw flexing.

Blue light ran down Aaron's face. "Is she okay?"

"Aaron," Theo started.

Kade winced. Theo's tone was too obvious, too *apologetic* to mean anything but what Aaron was dreading. Aaron picked up on it in an instant, expression hardening as he whirled around.

"I'm okay, by the way," Kade called. "If you were worried."

Aaron shuddered. For a moment he stilled, looking at Kade's intact chest with something sickeningly close to relief. Then Aaron turned back, pushing through the throng.

Theo surged after him, dragging him into a dark, empty hallway near the main entrance.

Aaron shoved at Theo's iron grip. "Get off me!"

Theo ignored him. "Just tell us what the plan is."

Aaron glowered. "How many times do I have to say it? I. Can't. *Tell*. You."

"And you wouldn't even if you could, got it," Kade said over the thumping music. "While we're doing unanswerable questions, why don't you have the crossbow hand? Is it in the bag? If I had a crossbow hand I'd wear it *all* the time."

Aaron ripped his arm out of Theo's grip. This time, Theo let him.

"I wish you *did* have the crossbow hand, Renfield," Aaron snarled. "I wish you got *all* of this. I wish—"

He stopped, snapping his teeth shut. His green eyes shone with fearful tears, and Kade was struck once again by the same festering, uncomfortable pity that Aaron had triggered these past few months.

"I shouldn't have come," Aaron muttered, clutching the duffel bag strap. "I should—I have to go."

He turned for the door.

Theo grabbed his arm again. "Aaron."

Aaron whirled around and shoved him bodily up against the wall.

Kade started forward, adrenaline spiking as he imagined hidden knives, arrows, a crossbow that popped out if you pressed a button. But Theo looked at him pointedly, the obvious hitting Kade as he came to a stop: Aaron couldn't shove Theo into a wall unless he let him.

Aaron was obviously having the same realization. He laughed, the noise echoing jagged and ugly around the hallway.

"I was always jealous of you. Always thought you were what..." Aaron stopped, a twisted version of that loathsome smile Kade hated for so long spreading over his face. "What my dad really wanted."

Theo hesitated. "I thought the same thing about you sometimes."

"Yeah. Well." Aaron laughed again, green eyes gleaming. "Here's to disappointing our parents."

Theo's mouth twitched. Almost laughing with him, Kade realized.

Aaron let him go and slumped out of the hall, the duffel bag weighing heavy around his neck.

Kade watched him walk out the main entrance. Beverly Sloan stepped aside to let him through.

"He's going to the tree," he said. "Right?"

"I don't know where else he'd—" Theo broke off as feedback screeched over the speakers. Kade and Theo curled inwards, slapping their hands over their ears. It was like nails on a chalkboard, but inside their skulls.

The feedback stopped. Finn's voice echoed through the house: "Welcome, girls and ghouls and fangy fools!"

"Where the hell is he?" Theo growled.

He took off toward the living room. Kade followed, glancing back to watch Aaron vanish into the woods surrounding the house.

Lights raced over the living room, illuminating plastic scars and fake blood as they pushed through the crowd.

Finn's voice boomed through the house, deep and impossible to track: "I hope everybody's ready for a monster mash! Things are getting wild in this bitch. I might not be in the room, but I'm *watching*...and the best monster gets a prize that's to *die* for!"

A cheer rose. Kade tried not to flinch. The doom was back with a vengeance, his stomach twisting with it. Like watching his dad get louder and louder at the dinner table when he was a kid, that inexorable dread. *Something bad is going to happen.*

Kade leaned as close to Theo as he dared. "We should light a fire."

"What?"

"Get everyone out," Kade explained. "We could go into the kitchen while everyone's distracted. That's a realistic place for fires to start. We could totally get away with that."

Theo stopped. His eyes were closed, frowning as he concentrated.

Kade stepped on his foot. "Oi!"

Theo shushed him. His head was cocked. Listening for Finn's voice. His *real* voice, not the tinny echo broadcasting from the speakers.

Kade didn't dare join him. The heartbeats were too loud.

"This way," Theo said, and took off toward the cordoned-off rooms that lay beyond the party areas.

Kade cursed and followed. He wanted to tell Theo to slow down, to wait, to point out they hadn't even danced yet, they could at least spare one last dance in this horror show of a last night on earth—

Then he froze and inhaled deeply.

Blood. Just a speck of it, far too close. A drop, barely noticeable through the crush of heat and sweat and face paint.

Theo ducked into the hallway.

Kade turned.

Blond curls behind a bright white volto mask. An impeccably pristine woman strode toward him, lifting her hand out of her cape.

The scent hit him like a shovel. Kade jerked back. But it was too late: Carol Fairgood grabbed his face and rubbed her bloody thumb over his lips.

And Kade forgot about everything. He forgot Theo. Forgot Aaron and Felicity and Finn. Forgot everything that wasn't the woman retreating toward an open window. He heard himself snarl as he pushed warm bodies out of the way, ignoring their yelps.

They didn't matter.

Nothing mattered but following the scent of blood out the window into the dark night.

Into the forest.

CHAPTER
TWENTY-THREE

FINN'S BEDROOM door was locked.

Theo grabbed the knob and crushed it, shoving the door open. "Harley!"

Finn jumped up from his computer chair, almost tripping over his cape in the process. His face was painted white. His red lips broke into a nervous grin when he saw Theo's thunderous expression.

"You're not rocking your monster skin," he said. "You know I can kick you out of the party for that, right?"

He bared his plastic fangs. Theo wanted to punch that giddy smile off his face. Kade might die tonight, for good this time. The town might go down with him. And here was Finn, bouncing in his stupid plastic cape. He had a speaker set up on his computer desk and a huge monitor showing a bird's-eye view of the dancefloor. He also had a dead aloe plant on his nightstand, which only made Theo even more furious. Aloe plants were one of the easiest plants to take care of, and this asshole had let it rot.

"You really want to get back out there," Finn continued. "Big finale coming up."

"What's the prize?" Theo barked.

Finn's grin slipped. He had finally noticed his broken door. "Whoa, what the hell?"

Theo charged him, slamming him effortlessly up against the wall. "What's. The. *Prize*? What was in that bag you dug up with my mom?"

"Your mom?" Finn said, voice ratcheting up several pitches. "I don't know anything about your mom!"

Theo punched him in the stomach.

Finn folded like a wet paper towel. He stared up at Theo, eyes wet, face slowly going red.

"*Dude*," he choked. He held up his hands. He was always like this, even in middle school: all his bravado vanished the second someone dared call him out on his bullshit. It was why he never rose in the popularity ranks until both Theo and Aaron were taken out of the running.

Theo glanced toward the door. He couldn't hear Kade following him. He'd been right behind Theo, right?

He looked at the screen showing the dancefloor. No commotion, no screaming, just teenagers busting a move in monster makeup. Whatever had distracted Kade, it wasn't the chaos they were waiting for.

Finn touched his arm cautiously. "L-look, man—"

Theo turned back and shook him. "The bag you pulled out of the woods, what'd you do with it?"

"I..." Finn blinked, dazed. "Y-your mom said I could have it, man. You can have some, I'm gonna keep some of it anyway. Whoever wins the prize isn't going to know."

"What the hell are you talking about?" Theo changed tactics. "What did they promise you?"

Finn spluttered. "My parents?"

Theo bared his teeth, letting them sharpen into fangs. "You see me growling, Finn? I will bite your goddamn throat out. What did they promise you, you *idiot*?"

"Oh wow those are cool," Finn said in a rush. He giggled fearfully. "*Shit*. You really went all in when you started dating Monster, huh?"

Theo bit a chunk out of his shoulder.

Finn's giggle became a shriek. He writhed against Theo's grip, kicking uselessly.

"WHAT THE HELL IS WRONG WITH YOU?" he sobbed. "IT'S MY *BIRTHDAY*, YOU LITTLE FREAK!"

Theo slammed his head into the wall. "What the *hell* is going on, Harley?"

"Okay! Okay! I'll tell you!" Finn gasped, blood leaking into his shirt. "Y-your mom promised me an internship at her law firm over the summer! A-and maybe she'll give me some of your inheritance?"

Theo stared at him. Finn was curled up and sniveling, shaking in Theo's grip.

"She said she wanted to surprise you," Finn cried. "She said you loved surprises, that she'd make everything up to you!"

Theo swallowed the bitter taste in his mouth. "And the bag?"

"Moonshine," Finn blurted. "It's super old, really potent! Your mom spiked the punch for me! I'm going to give half the bag to whoever wins the costume contest!"

"My *mom* spiked the punch?" Theo repeated, incredulous. He turned again, watching teens stumble and sway on the monitor.

So they'll be useless in a fight, Theo realized with dawning horror. His hand tightened unconsciously in Finn's shirt.

I wanted to see what you'd do, Victor had told him once. Finn was a test. A *distraction.* Every time, his dad set a trap. And Theo had walked into it like an idiot, every single time. Still dancing on his father's strings.

He set Finn down with a thump.

Finn made a wet noise, every sweaty inch of him trembling. "What are you? Did you kidnap the Emmerson siblings? Did you *kill* Skeeter Bass?"

Theo sighed. He didn't have time for this. He had to find Kade.

He grabbed Finn's shoulders, ignoring Finn's terrified meep.

"Something terrible is going to happen," Theo announced. "I need you to get everybody the hell out of here. Blast it on the speakers, take away the punch, turn the lights on. Get them out. *Now*."

Finn stared at him, blood and tears and snot dripping down his chin.

"But it's the party of the year," he said weakly.

An ear-splitting scream ripped through the house. Finn jumped, and Theo caught the scent of a not inconsiderable amount of pee.

Another yell accompanied it, pained and fierce.

"FAIRGOOD," Beverly Sloan screamed. "GET HERE, NOW!"

"Shit," Theo spat, and ran.

The party was in chaos. Teenagers in monster masks screaming, running, crashing into each other as they tried to escape. *Dance until you die,* sang Finn's prerecorded voice in shoddy autotune. *D-d-dance until you d-d-die.*

Theo saw Russel first. Crouching in front of a shattered window, holding a freshman's arms down while he fed.

Theo tackled him. They slammed into the wall, Russel thankfully releasing his grip on the crying freshman.

"It's me," Theo growled as Russel snarled and swiped. "Hey! Quit it!"

A rope of fire eye descended around Russel's neck. Beverly Sloan yanked him back, not even looking at Russel as he clawed at his smoking restraints. She was too busy aiming her crossbow at a feral Ryan Emmerson, who was trying to bite Skeeter's finger off.

She squeezed the trigger. Ryan Emmerson jerked, unlatching their fangs from Skeeter's hand as an arrow exploded through their shoulder.

"Your boyfriend's missing," Beverly told Theo.

He didn't reply. He had finally spotted Milly, who was chasing a guy from Theo's math class into the kitchen, her hair a tangled mess, her eyes solid black. And Delilah Emmerson, who was feasting on an adult chaperone as their daughter screamed and sprayed her with pepper spray, which made the adult choke and Delilah roar in annoyance.

But the worst was Sundance. She was on the ceiling, digging her nails into the wood. Her head twisted, meeting Theo's gaze. There was no gruff understanding in her eyes. No amused twinkle. Just black.

He couldn't see Felicity. He supposed that was for the best. She was lethal when she was human, he didn't particularly want to see what she could do as a starving, feral vampire.

"Theo," Beverly prompted. She yanked Russel's fire eye chain tighter, making Russel yowl and tear at the ropes. Any more ripping and he'd break free.

"You need to go," Beverly continued, raising her crossbow at a charging Ryan Emmerson. "Now!"

Theo shot up. He wanted to stay, to fight, to *protect*. But Kade was gone, which meant that there was much worse happening in the forest. He was playing right into their hands and he knew it. But that bone-deep doom that had been haunting Kade his whole life was finally catching up to him. Theo wasn't going to let him face it alone.

Beverly shot a second time. Another arrow burst through Ryan's leg, making them stumble to the ground.

"Nonlethal," Theo reminded her.

She gave him a thunderous look. Not about the reminder, Theo realized. She hadn't seen Felicity, either.

A ripping noise made them both look down. Russel had broken free of his fire eye rope and was blurring to his feet, his fangs bared.

Beverly bared her teeth back. It made her look so much like her daughter that Theo had the bizarre urge to laugh. She leveled her crossbow at him just as Ryan picked up speed behind her.

Theo cursed, readying himself to leap. But before he could, a dirty bottle spun out of nowhere and smashed into Russel's head, knocking him sideways.

Finn Harley stood in the hallway door, tears streaming down his cheeks as the partygoers ran around him.

"Jump shot, asshole," he squeaked. Any sense of pitiful triumph in his voice was shattered when Sundance slammed into him from above, pinning him to the ground and ripping into his already-bleeding cheek.

Theo stared out over the carnage: Sundance feeding. Classmates screaming and fleeing. Skeeter leaping onto Ryan Emmerson, jabbing her bleeding fingers into their eyes. The pepper-spray freshman attacking Delilah Emmerson with the bottle of moonshine Finn Harley had jump-shotted at Russel. And Russel being looped into yet another fire eye lasso as Beverly reloaded her crossbow.

"Go," Beverly ordered, taking aim at Sundance. "We'll take care of this."

She didn't say the next thing. She *couldn't* say it. But the plea was obvious in her voice.

"I'll get her back," Theo promised.

Then he ran.

TWENTY-FOUR

THE SCENT *of burned flesh hangs in the air long after Kade stops screaming.*

Theo cups Kade's scorched cheek. Even his eyelashes burned when that last hunter struck the match. Betraying them, just as Kade whispered they would.

Useless, Theo thinks as he rubs Kade's ashen cheekbone, smearing the blood of the hunters he'd been able to catch while the rest of them fled into the woods. Kade was just beyond the tree when they set him alight. Even if Kade were touching the gnarled thing, it wouldn't matter. It has to be Theo's burn.

"This wasn't the plan," he hears himself say.

"Quite," says a disappointed voice behind him.

Theo doesn't bother looking up. He knows what he will find: Victor scowling down at him, his plan foiled.

"You are useless now," Victor continues. "A knife without a lamb. A lock without a key."

Theo waits for the end. It hardly matters now. He has no

interest in eternity if Kade isn't beside him. His eyes burn with black tears, ready to spill over.

Victor sighs. "Never you mind, boy. We'll do better next time. Distract the high-and-mighty hunters. Do a better job with you."

This is what finally makes Theo lift his gaze from Kade's beloved, burned face. "What do you—?"

He never finishes the sentence.

The last thing he sees before Victor rips Theo's head off his shoulders is a black tear dripping off Theo's chin and landing—

—on Kade's cheek.

Kade gasped in pain, his crying forgotten as he jolted back to himself. He was tied to the gnarled tree. Fire eye thorns bit through his shirt and his shins, tiny bolts of agony rushing through him whenever he dared to move.

Victor Fairgood stood in front of him. He was in his human form, wearing the same clothes Kade had seen him wear in the vision. They were moth-eaten and worn, but otherwise intact.

"Hello rabbit," Victor said gently. "Here we are again. Are you ready?"

Kade blinked back a fresh wave of tears, Theo's two-hundred-year-old grief looming over him.

"Am I the rabbit or the lamb?" he croaked.

"All prey animals are alike to me," Victor replied smoothly.

A wet nose brushed his arm. Kade jerked and saw

Sparky's big red eyes gazing at him. She gave him an apologetic lick and butted her head against him.

"Heel," Victor said.

Sparky went rigid. She walked back to Victor, paws shaking with the effort of trying to hold herself back. She sat down next to him with her ears flat against her head.

A growl reverberated through the trees. For a second Kade thought it was Sparky, but her muzzle didn't move.

The growling grew louder. Victor stepped aside to reveal Felicity writhing in the dirt behind them. Her arms and feet were bound, her skin torn and smoking from trying to escape.

"Liss!" Kade's cold heart sank.

Felicity's head snapped up, black eyes boring into him. She growled louder.

"The rest are at the party," Victor said, stroking a long line down Sparky's back. "I kept her back. She's a real firecracker."

Kade squeezed his eyes shut, imagining a pack of feral vampires descending on Finn's stupid party. Some of them had never had blood, and they'd been turned for over a week. What was that desperation like?

Victor stepped closer, watching Kade with a strange intensity. "He turned you. That's smart. But I bet he didn't expect all that savageness." Victor pressed his gloved finger over the rope on Kade's stomach. "It's *in* you. Not many vampires feel it as pure as you. You'd make a lethal member of my coven."

Kade couldn't help it: he snarled. Gnashed his teeth like he'd done so many times at school, only this time he had the fangs to back it up.

Victor smiled. He pressed harder, and Kade's snarl broke off into a pained gasp as the fire eye bit through the fabric.

"It's almost a shame you have to die," Victor continued. He cocked his head, scanning the tree line. "Honey?"

Carol Fairgood came stumbling out of the trees. Her mask was gone. A circlet of twigs and holly balanced carefully on her curls. She was wearing the dress Kade recognized from the sketches: tattered and white, with a fanged belt that would've made Kade jealous in a less perilous situation. The spear was balanced flat between her hands. Pink flowers were knotted around the handle, gleaming in the moonlight.

She looked like an offering, Kade realized. Like a sacrifice. All the trust of a dozy piglet in its owner's arms, not noticing the knife in the other hand.

Victor took the spear from her and pressed a kiss to her forehead. "You've done wonderfully, my love. Everything I asked and more. If only everyone was as obedient."

Kade shivered. Something was moving behind his still heart. A *pull*.

Theo Fairgood blurred to a stop between the trees.

Sparky whined, jerking one paw out toward him. Then Victor clicked his tongue and Sparky stilled.

Victor petted her and turned to Theo. "I don't suppose I can convince you to do as you're told? There's still time, you know. All your mistakes will be wiped clean. We can be a family, a proper one this time."

Theo didn't look away from Kade. They both knew what was coming next. Everyone had agreed. But none of them knew what would happen after.

Theo opened his mouth. "I'll—"

An arrow sailed out of the trees. It embedded in Victor's chest.

For a moment, no one moved. Then a horrifying noise ripped out of Victor's throat, his back bowing and his legs straining as he grew into that white spindly monster from the woods.

"Protect this," he told Carol, pushing the flower-knotted spear into her hands.

Theo rushed forward and pulled at Kade's bindings. He yanked, hissing as the fire eye ropes burned his hands down to the bone.

Mrs. Fletcher barreled through the trees, an ax in each hand. "Another!"

"I'm trying," came Aaron's urgent voice. He stepped into view, bruised and sweating, fumbling wildly with his crossbow hand.

Victor roared. His wings snapped out. He launched himself at Mrs. Fletcher, pinning her against a tree and tearing her neck open with his teeth.

Mrs. Fletcher screamed as blood splattered down her clothes. Her axes clattered to the dirt.

"MOM!" Aaron swung his crossbow hand around. A second arrow speared through Victor's chest. He jerked, but continued to feed.

Mrs. Fletcher raked him with her fingernails, scattering white skin flakes. "KILL THE OTHER ONES!"

Aaron hesitated. He was halfway through loading another crossbow.

Theo snapped the first rope around Kade's torso. Yanked one arm free.

"Theo," Kade warned.

"I know." Theo turned.

Aaron was aiming the crossbow straight at them. His eyes were huge and horrified. Kade felt sorry for him. He *hated* that he felt sorry for him. He had never liked the guy, even when they were sneaking around in the woods. But Aaron looked like he wanted to be anywhere else than the tail end of this story.

"You don't have to," Theo said.

Kade waited for Aaron's eyes to go dead. The decision made clear. For his face to flatten out into that same aloof, expressionless mask he'd been wearing since Kade met him. But his eyes didn't go dead. Kade had never seen Aaron more upset than when he reached for the trigger.

Theo's voice sharpened. "Aaron—"

"I'm sorry," Aaron whispered. Then his eyes caught on something and widened in horrified panic.

Felicity leapt on him with a roar. Aaron screamed as she tore open his throat, biting down so hard Kade heard something crack.

"*Shit*," Kade spat. He yanked at the rest of his bindings. His flesh burned, thorns digging into his skin.

Aaron was screaming, Mrs. Fletcher's yells were fading into pained whimpers, Sparky was trembling at Victor's side, Felicity was feral, and Carol was watching everything with such a look of genuine triumph Kade wanted to shake her, Felicity's bindings still hanging from her hands. She was still clutching that flowery spear, hugging it to her chest like Victor had given her a bouquet of roses.

"Theo," Kade whispered.

Theo nodded. It was time.

"I'll do it," Theo announced. "I'll burn him."

Victor stilled. He raised his face from Mrs. Fletcher's neck, jagged and dripping. Everything was quiet.

"You will?" Victor rasped.

Theo nodded. His hand tightened in Kade's shirt, which still had vines biting through it. He thumbed the fabric, the gentle touch filled with everything he couldn't say right now.

Kade wet his lips. They had to play into it.

"Theo," he whispered, letting every ounce of real worry bleed into his voice. "You can't...you're not..."

Theo took his free hand and slid Kade's glove off. Slowly, the way he did at the end of the day: Kade already in his pajamas, ready to climb into bed with a sheet between them.

"This is always how it was going to end," Theo said. "I'm sorry."

Kade wanted to tell him about the secondhand grief. How huge it had been, how intensely he'd felt his love, two hundred years gone. He wanted to tell Theo they'd done this all before, that this was the party where the hunters ambushed them. He wanted Theo to kiss him properly, charred lips be damned.

Theo raised Kade's bare hand to his lips and pressed a soft, burning kiss to his palm.

The veins on Kade's palm flickered red. Not burning, but about to. The curse was preparing to complete itself. It would take root and spread through his whole body, burning him until he was ash and the door was sealed forever, the town saved.

Theo leaned back. The fire in Kade's veins died, leaving only a smoking kiss at the center of his hand.

Victor snarled, letting Mrs. Fletcher's unconscious body drop into the dirt. "What are you *doing*?"

Something snapped behind Kade's back.

Everybody went silent. Even Aaron, whose whimpers were fading as Felicity drained him. For a moment the only sound was the wet drag of Felicity feeding.

Another ear-splitting crack echoed through the forest. And another. Something inside the tree was breaking, the bark warping and bucking against Kade's back.

Victor eyed it warily. "What did you do?"

"What you said," Theo said quietly.

The burn on Kade's hand glowed a sickening black. The bark behind him pulsed, heating up.

Kade yanked at his bonds. "Theo!"

Theo darted forward. Victor didn't move. He was staring up at the tree, his face full of savage hope. His expression looked a lot like theirs, Kade noticed as Theo clawed through his bonds. Dooming the town for a chance to touch each other.

The last bond broke. Kade stumbled free just as the tree burst into flames.

Victor didn't look at them. He curled a wing over Carol's shoulders. "Come here, my love."

Carol's smile flinched as she stepped closer to the burning tree. She handed him the flower-laden spear, looking into her husband's pale face beseechingly. "I'll... I'll still be me. Right?"

Victor straightened the circlet in her blond curls. "And more, my love. Let your old spear enter you and regain every memory we had together."

Carol's smile steadied. She stepped closer.

"Don't," Theo blurted, jerking forward.

Sparky blocked his way, growling dangerously. Kade watched his leg come back. Then the inevitable faltering when he couldn't bring himself to hurt her.

"Mom," Theo yelled. "Don't do it!"

Victor cupped Carol's cheek. Then he thrust the spear through her stomach.

"MOM," Theo screamed.

She didn't look at him. Her white dress flowed with blood. Her mouth opened on a shuddery gasp, her hands braced on Victor's pale chest. She gazed up at him, full of pain and expectation and terrible love. Then she fell to the ground. Her heartbeat thudded to a stop.

Sparky's growls became whimpers.

Behind them, the tree started to cave in. Bits of bark collapsed, yanked inwards. Branch by branch.

A wet gurgle tore Kade's horrified gaze away. Aaron's bloody hand was in Felicity's hair. Not pulling, just cupping. If Kade ignored the gore, they almost looked like two lovers embracing.

"Come on," Kade said shakily, and took off toward Felicity and Aaron.

Theo stumbled after him. Kade pried Felicity off Aaron and pinned her to the ground, giving Theo the far more difficult task of leaning over a bleeding body without feeding.

"Failed," Aaron slurred. "We...we *failed*. You gotta... you need..."

He fumbled weakly for Theo's collar, smearing blood over the embroidered ferns.

"It's okay," Theo told Aaron as the flames raged behind them. He wedged a hand over the holes Felicity had gored into him, knitting the skin together. "We'll get you out of here, we'll regroup—"

But Aaron's eyes were slipping shut, his breathing slowing. The skin was regrowing, the blood was not.

Kade watched the realization dawn on Theo's face and knew what was going to happen next.

"Aaron," Theo croaked. He went to cut his wrist, to feed him the dead blood that would save his life.

Aaron batted him away weakly. "Don't you dare," he whispered. "I'd...I'd rather..."

His pale face went slack. His lifeless eyes flickered with reflected flames, staring at the one last thing he'd failed to stop.

Theo shook him. "Aaron. Hey!"

Victor raised a hand. The flames went out and the forest plunged into darkness.

"Theo," Kade whispered, unable to keep the fear out of his voice.

Victor flicked his hand. The coffin burst out of the ground. A charred body rose from its depths.

Kade shuddered, the movement so intense it jolted Felicity struggling under him. Long before he was born, Cyth had been right here. Burning. *Waiting*. And yet the clothes were not gone, the skin not melted. It was still a woman, if you squinted. The remains of a dress fused to the skin, patches of red, singed hair stuck to her scalp.

But only for a moment. Cyth's hair was growing. Thick and red and blazing, sprouting in great mounds and forming a plait that wrapped around her head like a crowd. Her burns cracked and fell away, revealing pink skin underneath. Sharp cheekbones. Dark, keen eyes.

Victor's breath hitched. A disbelieving smile spread over his face.

"My love," he breathed. "*Finally*."

THEO WATCHED in mute horror as Victor stepped over Carol's limp body to cup his beloved's cheeks. Aaron was still warm in his arms. Kade sat next to him, holding Felicity back from charging after the unconscious Mrs. Fletcher.

I'm gonna have to tell her what happened, Theo realized dully. He pressed harder, desperate and useless, on Aaron's wounds.

Victor nuzzled Cyth's hairline. "As beautiful as the day I lost you."

Cyth stared up at him, her dark eyes keen and wonderous. "I knew you'd come for me."

"Always," he vowed.

She cracked her neck. It extended horribly, her limbs lengthening, her skin growing even paler. Wings burst from her back. She smiled eagerly, her mouth full of fangs.

"We have a town to raze," she said. "But first, let's take care of your lock and key. We hardly need them now."

She turned toward Kade, who was still holding Felicity down. Her gaze was dismissive, the same way everyone's gaze was dismissive when it came to Kade "Monster" Renfield. Like Kade wasn't Theo's whole world.

Theo roared.

It went on and on, splintering in his throat.

"Ah," Victor said quietly. "Finally."

Theo dropped Aaron and stood. His bones lengthened, his skin stretched and turned white. Wings tore out of his back, huge and horrible.

"Theo," Kade whispered.

Theo ignored him, shaking his wings out with a hiss. He'd been searching for the monster inside him, and he'd finally found it.

If he looked at Kade, he would see the horror on his face. The wrongness of watching the love of his life turn into something unrecognizable. But Theo was too focused on Cyth, who was watching him transform with detached curiosity.

Theo screeched. Then he flared his wings and streaked toward Cyth.

Victor clicked his tongue. "Attack."

Sparky leapt to intercept Theo, a rush of black fur and sorrowful red eyes.

Theo tried to slow down, but he was already in

midair. He slammed into Sparky, sending them rolling into a tree. Theo shielded Sparky with his wings, taking the brunt of the blow. Then they were struggling in the dirt, Sparky snapping at his face, whining all the while.

Theo blocked her, letting her sink her teeth into his unnaturally long arm.

"It's me," he said, his voice strange and rough. "Hey! We worked on this! I *know* you. You're not his. You don't want to hurt me, you don't want to hurt *anybody*."

Sparky growled, trembling. She forced her teeth deeper into his arm, even as she whimpered. Trying to wrest herself free.

Theo gritted his fangs against the pain. He used the leverage to drag her closer, fixing his eyes on hers. "You don't want to hurt anybody," he repeated.

Sparky's jaw relaxed. She spasmed, then jerked back, licking furiously at Theo's wounds.

Theo slumped, stroking her head. "There we go. We're not his. He made us, but that doesn't make us his. We—"

Theo stopped. He'd spent this whole time thinking he needed to be vicious to win this fight. To become what his father always told him. Both times he escaped these fights, it wasn't because he was vicious. The first time, it was because he recognized a fire eye plant while he was bleeding out. Because Kade distracted Hawthorn at just the right moment. The second time, it was because the Sloans came in to save the day.

Sparky kept licking the tooth marks as Theo's skin

turned pinker. His limbs shortened once more, wings shriveling back into his shoulders. Human again. Or as close as he could get.

Theo tipped his head back and yelled with every ounce of hope he had left in him: "HELP! WE'RE HERE! HELP US!"

Kade cursed as he watched Sparky and Theo tumble into the tree.

"Now would be a great time for you to come back," he told Felicity, who was unhappily pinned under him.

She thrashed, trying to bite his arm.

"Or not," Kade said shakily.

Theo yelled from the trees. Calling for help. Victor looked back at him, annoyed. He stepped toward him.

"Not yet," Cyth told him. She was still moving languidly toward Kade. Other than a faint wildness in her eyes, she hadn't changed from the woman he'd seen in the visions. This wasn't her first time being trapped for generations.

Kade shivered under her gaze and lowered to hiss in Felicity's ear: "*Hey*. I need you on my team right now, or we're screwed. I need knife-throwing Liss, not out of her mind with bloodlust Liss. You already ate one guy, stop being greedy."

He glanced over at Aaron's body, guilt coursing through him. This was going to destroy her.

The scent of fresh blood hit Kade in a wave.

Cyth was dragging Mrs. Fletcher's unconscious body over. Her head was cocked, watching him twitch as she dropped her bleeding body a foot away.

"There is an admirable monster in these two," she told Victor. She knelt to meet Kade's gaze, smiling when he shrank back. Her eyes were so *dark*. He'd never seen her with normal eyes, even in the visions. It was as if this was her true self, and any human form was a disgrace.

"She is still settling," she said, wings folding neatly behind her. "But *you*—it is in you, is it not? Deep as bones. Deep as soul. You've known you're a monster long before you were given fangs."

Kade held his breath. But he could still smell it: rich blood, pulsing sluggishly from the holes in Mrs. Fletcher's neck. She'd tried to kill him. She *did* kill him. If anyone deserved to be drained, it was her. Right?

"You could join us," Cyth continued in that soft, scraping voice. "I can feel how much you hate this town. Wouldn't you like revenge for all it's done to you?"

Kade swallowed. The hunger howled inside him, almost as deafening as Mrs. Fletcher's slowing heartbeat. Watching the town burn down was one of his go-to fantasies in freshman year. Whenever he'd been pushed to the ground or barked at in the hallway or Aaron ignored him again, he'd imagine pushing a drum of gasoline under the gym and setting a match.

It would be satisfying. But Kade was so tired of being the town monster.

Felicity went rigid underneath him. Her eyes were wide with panic, twisting to see who was on top of her.

"Where are we?" she slurred. "What happened? Why is Aaron's mom—?" She froze as she noticed Cyth and Victor's monstrous forms.

Cyth waved a clawed hand. "Hello, vampling. Would you like to join us?"

Felicity barked an outraged laugh. "Would you like to shut the hell up?"

Kade clambered off her and pulled her to her feet. They needed to find the others. Regroup. But first, they needed to get Theo and get the hell out. This wasn't a fight they could win, not with three of them—

"HEY!"

Kade turned.

Theo stood in the splinters of the tree he'd crashed into. No wings, no pale, sleeting skin—he was once more the boy Kade had fallen in love with. Sparky stood at his side, tail wagging.

"You're very loud tonight," Victor called. "I heard your pathetic little cry for help. It's like all those years of parenting never happened."

"It happened," Theo replied coolly, hands in fists at his sides. "I'll probably still be recovering from it when I'm a hundred."

"Well, I don't see..." Victor trailed off as vampires emerged from the trees.

Ryan Emmerson, their eyes bleeding black. Delilah Emmerson at their side, teeth bared.

Sundance with moonshine glass studding her bare arms, Skeeter carrying two axes at once and panting nervously. Milly with a bloody mouth, her facial scar healed. Interestingly, her eye had not. It was still flat white, staring through the smoke unwaveringly.

Russel covered in fire eye burns and carrying Beverly Sloan, who had a giant duffel bag in her lap and a crossbow leveled at Victor's heart.

Cyth inclined her head. "Minions. I see your appetite has been whetted. The night only gets better from here."

"Oh, shut it," Sundance snarled. "And while you're at it, get the hell away from those kids."

Victor laughed. "What *is* this, Theo?"

Theo's shoulders sagged. Kade could see it in him, the same thing he'd see if he was looking in a mirror: Theo was tired of being a monster, too.

"Let's end this story already," Theo said.

Victor's wings spasmed, his mouth twisting in a snarl. "You really think that I'm going to let some ragtag band of vamplings take me down after I finally achieved what I set out to do two hundred years ago?"

"I don't think you're going to *let* me do anything," Theo said. "I think—"

An anguished cry cut them off. Felicity was on her knees next to Aaron, cradling his bloody face. She raised his shaky red hand to her mouth. For a moment Kade thought she was going to lick it.

Then she looked up, peeling her lips back into a ferocious snarl.

"I'm going to FUCKING kill you," she screamed at Victor.

Then she leapt. Everybody leapt with her, weapons drawn.

Kade landed on Victor's wings and started ripping. Victor screamed and bucked, trying to shove him off. Then Skeeter's ax slammed into his elbow and he turned to swipe at her instead.

Something burned Kade's cheek. He whirled to see Beverly tossing him one end of a fire eye net.

"Pin them down," she barked. "Let's see how they like being prey for once."

Kade grabbed the net, clenching his jaw as it singed his palms. He wrapped it around Victor's wings and threw it around Victor's front where Theo was waiting.

Victor roared. His burned arm flashed out, and the net tore.

"Another," Theo barked.

Kade caught the next net. And the next. His hands smoked, the air filling with the stench of burned flesh as they wound net after net around Cyth and Victor. First their wings were trapped. Then their legs. Kade ducked and weaved and lunged, getting a claw in the face and Ryan Emmerson's leather-clad elbow slammed into his nose as they gained ground.

Beverly stood back, firing arrow after arrow into the increasingly trapped monsters. Felicity screamed, gouging chunks out of them with her claws. Skeeter's ax buried itself in Cyth's shoulder, Russel's claws slashed her cheek open, Milly shoved a shard of moonshine glass in Victor's eye.

"Catch," Theo yelled.

Kade turned. Theo was dragging a can of gasoline from Beverly's bag, eyes on him as he threw.

Kade caught it and poured it over Victor's head.

Victor spat out a mouthful of foul liquid and shrieked. His trapped leg struck out and snapped the net pinning it down.

"Liss," Kade yelled, and threw.

Felicity caught it in midair. She splashed gasoline into Cyth's arrow-studded torso. Liquid leaked into her black intestines.

Cyth lunged at her, teeth tearing through the net and searing her gums.

Felicity ducked out of the way and tossed the gasoline to Skeeter.

Nets snapped. More nets piled on. Gasoline flowed, tossed from person to person until Cyth and Victor were dripping with it.

"Kade," Theo panted. "Lighter."

Kade fumbled the silver lighter out of his pocket. He'd polished it last night, like always.

Victor snarled up at them from the dirt. His wings were trapped against his back, the fire eye net binding him tight against a struggling Cyth.

"Going to have to be vicious," he told Theo as

Sundance poured one more splash of gasoline over their writhing bodies. "If you want to kill me, you'll have to become the very thing I always—"

Theo cut him off. "Victor. Shut up."

Kade threw the lighter.

The forest lit up. Inhuman screams rang through the trees. Kade averted his eyes as they thrashed, only to find that Theo was doing the same thing.

"This is taking too long," Felicity growled. She grabbed an ax from Beverly and strode up to the flaming vampires.

Theo flinched. Kade touched his sleeve, instinctually making sure not to get too close to his bare hand.

"Felicity," Milly said, slurring around her fangs. "We should pick—"

Felicity heaved the ax down. Then again. And again. It took five in total for the screams to go silent. The vampires' heads rolled onto the forest floor, still smoldering.

"There," Felicity said shakily. "D-done."

She swayed on the spot. Then she collapsed. Beverly and Skeeter ran to her side.

Kade looked at Theo, confused.

"He sired her," Theo reminded him. "Kill your sire and turn human again."

Kade squeezed his eyes shut. "Right. Shit."

He stared at Felicity's lax body a moment longer, then tugged at Theo's sleeve. "Come on."

Kade led him away from the bodies. Away from an

unconscious Felicity, whose heart was starting to beat once more. Away from their classmates bleeding black and Russel doing his best to craft an eyepatch for Ryan Emmerson while their newly gouged eyes grew back in. Away from Mrs. Fletcher, who was starting to moan. Away from Theo's mom lying motionless on the ground. They would have to do something about them all—but not right now.

Kade led him into the trees and turned to face him. Black blood was drying in Theo's hair. Burns covered his arms. He was so beautiful Kade ached.

Theo gestured at Kade's cheek. "You have something."

"Come and get it then," Kade whispered.

Theo took off one glove and reached up. His fingertips were cool and lovely as they stroked the grime away, and Kade marveled. He'd been starving for such a simple touch for so long.

Theo cupped Kade's face. He watched Kade with disbelief and wonder, like he had never felt anything as glorious as Kade's sharp cheekbones. He pressed their foreheads together, nuzzled his nose. If Kade still had a heartbeat, it would have stuttered.

Then Theo kissed him. It was exhausted and bloody and sweet, everything Kade had been wanting for the last year.

The last seventeen years.

The last two hundred, depending on who you asked.

CHAPTER
TWENTY-SIX

FIFTY-THREE DAYS after Kade Renfield died, he watched the sun come up with his boyfriend.

It was his favorite part of the day. Dawn washing over Theo's curls, turning him even more glorious than usual.

Theo caught him looking and smiled. "Morning."

"Morning, sunshine," Kade replied softly. He shifted up the bed, burying his head in Theo's neck and wrapping his arms around him. Theo stroked his angular shoulders, humming contentedly. Most of their first proper night together had been like this: holding each other close, not daring to let go. They hadn't even gotten naked. Even after all that build up, double-dead parents really harshed the vibe. For the first night, anyway.

Theo kissed Kade's split eyebrow. "It's Saturday. What do you want to do?"

Kade hummed. They already had their homework finished. They'd completed everything on their to-watch list. Kade had no craft projects lined up and no shifts at Milly's bookstore until tomorrow afternoon.

"How about a hike?" he suggested. "Might get lucky and find some puffball mushrooms."

"Sure. Do we invite the others?"

Before Kade could reply, the doorknob clicked. They waited. Sure enough, Sparky pushed the door open, wagging triumphantly at her trick.

"Hey girl," Theo said as she jumped up onto the bed. "Want to come on a hike?"

Kade watched him scruff her ears, an ease flowing through him which he'd never known before this summer. It was never for long, a handful of seconds at most. Sundance on the couch singing along to the *MASH* theme song, her knee bumping his. Flying through the woods, warm wind on his face. Theo kissing his bare knuckles.

But as always, the ease ended. A spark of hunger jolted through him, so intense he had to close his eyes. He *was* getting better. But most days the hunger was just as bad as on that very first day, digging his nails through his jeans so he didn't start feeding on Sundance right there in the living room.

Theo touched his arm. "Babe? You okay?"

Kade pulled up a smile. "I gotta go see a microwave about some deer blood. Want any?"

Theo shook his head.

"More for me." Kade kissed Theo's cool wrist and slid out of bed to find clothes. "Don't wait up."

Theo stroked Sparky, watching him get dressed in silence right up until the end. Then he said, "You fixed your shirt."

Kade looked down at the shirt he'd just put on. It was the same one he'd worn to Finn's party. The fire eye had punctured a line through the middle, so Kade had sliced it into a crop top. The last part of the phrase was gone. Now it just read *U STAY SOFT*.

Theo touched the hem, ghosting his fingers over the letters.

"Suits you," he said.

He ran into Sundance in the kitchen. She was on the ceiling, muttering as she scrubbed a stubborn spot of water damage.

"Hey," he called up to her as he fetched a container of deer blood from the fridge. "We're going on a hike. Wanna come?"

"Rain check," she replied. "I've been meaning to clean this crap for years. I'm doing the gutters next."

"Suit yourself," Kade replied. He started to grab a mug from the cabinet. Then he paused and put the full container in the microwave. He would've gone back for seconds anyway, no use wasting a mug.

Sundance floated down. Other than an aversion to hunting, she'd adapted well to the vampire lifestyle. She liked having more time to get things done. She was even looking into night classes. *Poetry*, of all things. Kade never knew she was interested.

She wrapped him in an inhumanly tight hug. Yet another thing that had changed since they died: every time she saw Kade, he got a hug. *Life's too short to not hug your kid,* she liked to say. Then, if he was around, she'd hug Theo.

"Home later?" she asked into his shoulder. "I'm up to your favorite seasons of *MASH*. BJ's arrived and Frank is gone."

"The sweet spot," Kade muttered. He kissed her forehead and leaned back, one eye on the microwave timer. "Count on it. We won't be long."

Aunt Sundance gave him another fond squeeze. Then she floated back up to the ceiling with her washcloth.

Kade sent a message to the LockSuckers group chat at eight in the morning. An hour later, four of them had shown up to their hike: Felicity, idly throwing knives into trees as she walked. Skeeter, who was admiring the birds. Ryan Emmerson, who was taking advantage of not being able to feel the heat by wearing layers and layers of leather.

And Russel, who still hadn't worked out what emojis meant, and had eggplant-reacted to the hiking invitation. He and Theo were lingering at the back of the group, distracted by local fauna.

Kade took a sip from his thermos and nudged Skeeter, who was watching Felicity fiddle with fire eye up ahead. "How is she?"

"Um," Skeeter said. "She's okay? We had a good talk last night. Then she freaked out and started smashing up the garage. But she cleaned it up after."

"Whoo," Kade said faintly.

"Whoo," Skeeter agreed, eyes fixed on Felicity twisting the thorny fire eye vine around her fingers. Skeeter had moved back in with her shocked parents after Finn's party, but she spent most of her sleepless nights at Felicity's place, discussing chess and training and some-times convincing Felicity to go to bed before three a.m.

Felicity wasn't taking her brief stint as a vampire well. She trained until she collapsed, gaining back all the scars that dying had wiped clean. At first Kade thought it was guilt over Aaron. Then he'd caught her watching them. She'd see Skeeter scale a tree or Theo fly up to retrieve an ax or watch Sundance feed and she'd get this look on her face that had nothing to do with guilt. It was *longing*. She missed being a vampire, even if her vampirism had been so terrible and bloody. The only one who got to turn human when Victor died and the only one who might've chosen this undead life anyway.

She hadn't brought it up with the boys yet. But Kade had heard her whispering with Skeeter. She was thinking about getting Skeeter to turn her after graduation.

"My ears are burning," Felicity called from up ahead, threading the fire eye around her wrist.

"Just talking about what a sore loser you are," Skeeter replied.

Felicity barked a laugh. "*Moi*? Have you *met* yourself? Last time I won a game of chopsticks you threatened to cut my hair off!"

Skeeter pointed to the tree line marking the end of the woods. "Race you."

Felicity laughed and tucked the fire eye into her pocket. "Eat my dust."

Skeeter took off. Felicity ran after her. She was no match. But she gave it her all, arms pumping, heart rate climbing as she chased Skeeter through the trees.

Ryan Emmerson came over from their detour to take a photo of a rotting log. They had gotten passionate about death and decay in the last few months, and were thinking about becoming a morgue technician.

"I'm annoyed I can't get tattoos," Ryan said. "Or if I dare take my earrings out, they close up immediately. I want a septum piercing but I don't want to re-pierce my nose every time I take it out."

Kade tugged at his crop top. "Preaching to the choir, baby goth. All my tattoo ideas are useless now."

"There must be a way," Ryan said determinedly, watching Felicity run. "If I knew the whole 'killing your sire turns you human again' schtick, *I* would've put my hand up."

Kade winced. "Heat of the moment. We just wanted them dead."

"Yeah, yeah." Ryan kicked a rock. It pinged off a tree twelve feet away. "Milly's vampire friend in North Carolina is doing research. No bites yet, but at least she's trying."

"That's awesome." Kade took another sip from his thermos, waiting. He recognized that nervous hunch. Ryan had more to say.

"Are you still thinking of going?" Ryan asked. "'Cause of the...?"

They trailed off, nodding at Kade's thermos of blood. None of the others needed to bring a thermos everywhere with them, just in case. Nobody else needed a babysitter when they drank human blood.

"Probably," Kade admitted. "Nobody in Tennessee knows how to help crazy newborns."

Ryan frowned. "You're not crazy."

Kade shrugged, watching Skeeter streak back toward them with Felicity in her arms.

Felicity climbed down, smirking. "Eat it, Bass. I'll beat you one day."

"In five hundred years, maybe," Skeeter replied.

Felicity blew her a kiss and mimed biting a chunk out of her chin. Then she paused, looking at the ruined greenhouse they were coming up to. The burned struts were still there, clumps of ash still sticking to the dirt.

The Fletcher house stood empty beyond it. Mrs. Fletcher hadn't bothered to sell it when she left town. Hadn't even packed. She just left, leaving the doors unlocked behind her.

Felicity glanced back at Kade, a silent question in her eyes. The fire eye wasn't back out again, but he could tell she was itching to start fidgeting again. If she turned into a vampire again, she would have to pick a new favorite thing to fiddle with.

Kade shrugged.

Felicity glared, letting him know how unhelpful he was being. Then she turned toward the others, flinging her arms up.

"Who wants to go hunting? I want some venison. Skeet, you'll carry it home for me, right?"

"Sure," Skeeter said warmly.

Felicity turned to Kade, expectant.

"Maybe later," Kade said.

Felicity nodded. She'd already gotten a thermos out, ready to fill it for Kade to drink later.

The others headed further into the forest. Theo appeared behind Kade, sliding an arm around his waist.

"You can go," Kade offered.

"I have food at home." Theo rubbed the strip of skin showing under Kade's crop top. Soothing him, but also checking to see if this was still allowed. Kade often found him watching the spot he was touching, waiting for Kade to blister.

They walked slowly, the burned flower patch

looming ahead. Kade waited to see if Theo was going to divert them, but Theo's footsteps were slow and certain. Like it wasn't Aaron's house through the trees and their past selves' bodies buried under the spot where Kade had bled out.

"Finn texted me," Theo said. "Wants to schedule another basketball session."

Kade sighed. "You heal a guy's bite marks *one* time, and now he won't leave you alone."

"Yeah, yeah. He's not as insufferable since his near-death experience." Theo kissed his cheek. "I heard you and Ryan talking back there."

Kade sighed louder. "Can't a guy have one private conversation on a vampire hike?"

"I can't help it," Theo said. "I'm tuned into you. You could go to the other side of the world and I'd still hear you."

Kade ducked his head, hiding his smile behind his thermos. Most of the curse's effects had gone away since they completed the ritual. But Theo could still sense him if he concentrated. Kade no longer had a heartbeat to listen to, but Theo still heard his voice louder than everyone else's.

They came up to the edge of the burned flower patch. Kade's lifeblood was gone, the scent covered by moss and dirt. Kade was surprised. For some reason he'd expected it to linger.

"I'll come with you," Theo offered.

Kade rolled his eyes. "We have school."

"Summer break soon," Theo pointed out. "And if things are still bad after graduation, I can take a gap year."

"You shouldn't put off college if I'm still having trouble in a *year*."

"Babe," Theo said. "I can go to college anytime. Not getting any older, remember?"

He gestured at himself. Theo Fairgood, eternally sixteen. His curls were still the exact same length they were the night of that fateful Founder's Day party. Even his clothes were similar: a pair of ironed jeans and a tight t-shirt. The only thing that had changed was his expression. No cockiness, no false bravado. His gaze was utterly unguarded. Nothing hiding the deep love he had for the boy in front of him.

Kade swallowed, throat suddenly thick. "You sure?"

Theo shrugged. "We have time."

"Yeah? You still gonna put up with me in five hundred years?"

"Four hundred," Theo replied instantly. "Then let's see other people."

Kade laughed wetly. Theo stepped close, leaning their forehead together.

"Kade," Theo said. "Love of my death. We'll watch the sun burn out."

They stood like that for a long time, surrounded by the forest that once haunted Kade's dreams, full of choking darkness and an inevitable death at the hands of the boy he loved. Now it was just trees.

It was strange, not being doomed anymore. Kade quite liked it.

It took a long time for Theo to pull back, a surprised noise rumbling in his throat.

"Wow," he said. "Look."

Kade followed Theo's pointing finger. Two pink flowers sat in the middle of the burned remains of the greenhouse, their stems twisting together. They were new, the petals not quite open. Still blooming.

Kade swallowed, blinking black liquid out of his eyes as he pictured the two boys curled underneath the dirt, a mirror of the boys standing on top of it.

"I thought they only bloomed one week a year," Kade said quietly.

"Must be magic." Theo kissed him again, long and deep. Then he stepped away. "Let's keep going. There's some really cool moss up ahead that I want you to see."

Kade grinned wetly, his grief replaced with a rush of wild joy. "With an offer like that, how can I refuse?"

Theo held out his hand.

Kade took it.

SPECIAL THANKS

Thank you so much for reading SOUL BURN! I hope you enjoyed the ride.

If you want to support me, please leave a review on Goodreads, Amazon and any social media of your choice.

You can get updates on my upcoming books by subscribing to my newsletter! Sign up by visiting my website at isbelleauthor.com. (by signing up you also get a free sapphic novella!)

You can also follow me on Tiktok @i.s.belle_writes or on Insta @isbelleauthor.

ACKNOWLEDGMENTS

To Jack McGee for fixing months of plot struggle with an hour-long conversation. It was one of my favorite hours of the entire year. I ran around the house high-fiving everyone and I rode that high for the rest of the day. I hope we never stop talking about made up shit, you brilliant bald bastard.

Next, let's give it up for my Kickstarter backers! I was blown away for the support this early-access campaign got. Let's go down the line:

Eden Mason, Milo N, Ashley Binder, Victoria P, Ary, Michelle B., Briar, Valentine, Ashleigh Wolfe, Bee Marie Chase, Lisa Herrick, Ayanna W, Ayla Peyrot, Ember, Maggie Callow, Persephone Embers, Katie Olive, Lucy Holland, Maddie Murray, Xander Beck, Kym Saunders, Hann K, Paige L, Katherine Nichols, JJ, Korvus F. M., Effy, Franchesca Caram, Michael Anthony, You, Steffi Happy, Mal M., Rowan Knight, Craig Esser, Marie C, Caitlyn Manning, Faith Dam, Gabriel De Jesus, Eric McCurry, kishaya wicks, Jor-Jor, Jess Autiero, Sophia, Maya Tohill, Jessica Williamson, DangerDays, Hailey Robinson, Clarissa, Finn, Virginia Queen, Gwyny Rankin, Stuart Turnbull, Jordie, Rafa

Apolo, Stephanie Lucas, Raul Alonso, Breaker Chitten-den, Millie, Phoenix, Gee Rothvoss, Fergus (the dear kitty cat), Jessi Heimer, C F Chan, Ashliicat, Noal, Urna Mukherjee, Nico, Lily Schnur, Rachiel Rosser, Chris Mobley, Rebekah Roennfeldt, Jack Schiller, Mish Phillips, Tara W, Tiffany Culver, Tayva Case, Dead Fish Books.

And of course my formatter, Edward Giordano, my cover artist Nani (shinirikaya on Insta), my editor Catriona Turner, and lastly my wonderful betas, Donna Taylor (author of the San Nico Slayers series) and Chloe Spencer!

ABOUT THE AUTHOR

I. S. Belle writes Young Adult and New Adult books that are sometimes spooky, often romantic, and always gay.

She works in a bookstore in New Zealand and stops to pat dogs in the street. If you have a dog and your local bookshop allows pets - for the love of booksellers, please bring them in.

She has a Creative Writing Masters from the International Institute of Modern Letters. You can find her on Tiktok @i.s.belle_writes or on Instagram @isbelleauthor.

ALSO BY I. S. BELLE

I. S. Belle

LGBT+ Young Adult Fiction

BABYLOVE SERIES

BABYLOVE

SUGARSNAP

SWEETHEARTS

ZOMBABE

ZOMBABE

HONEYBLOODS SERIES

HONEYBLOODS

HONEYBITES

HONEYCRAVES

BLOOD TETHERED SERIES

BLOOD TETHERED

VENOM BOUND

SOUL BURN

GIRLS NIGHT

GIRLS NIGHT